Jo Mazelis was born in S[...]
appeared widely in magazin[...]
also been broadcast on Radio[...]
to have received the Rhys D[...]
In addition to her writing she[...]
photographer. The cover [...]
Diving Girls are her own. She has lived and worked in
London and Aberystwyth.

She has a Welsh daughter and an American husband.
She lives on a hill in Swansea and has a very small view
of the sea.

PARTHIAN BOOKS

DIVING GIRLS

Jo Mazelis

PARTHIAN BOOKS

Parthian
The Old Surgery
Napier Street
Cardigan
SA43 1ED
www.parthianbooks.co.uk

©Jo Mazelis, 2002
All Rights Reserved

ISBN 1-902638-23-9
Typeset in Galliard by NW

Printed and bound by Dinefwr Press, Llandybie

With support from the Parthian Collective

The publishers would like to thank the Arts Council of Wales for
support in the publication of this volume

A cataloguing record for this book is available from the British
Library

Cover design & photography: Jo Mazelis

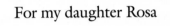

For my daughter Rosa

I would like to thank all of the following for their support and encouragement of my work. Without them I would have given up a long time ago: Lewis Davies, Robert Devcic, Brian Finnegan, John Goodby, Laurel Goss, Dr. Morag Hervey, Elin ap Hywel, Peter Mazelis, Robert Nisbet, Frances Nutt, Kevin Sinnott and Katy Train.

Stories

Forbidden Fruits

The Steadman women had elegance. Even from an early age, the two daughters seemed to possess some otherworldly grace that Mari could only dream of.

The daughters had long blonde straight hair that always hung sleekly and cleanly down their backs, and they walked gracefully, like models on a catwalk even though one of them was only nine and the other eleven. They had voices that seemed to be honey sweet and you never heard them curse or shriek. Not even if a wasp suddenly flew into their faces or they stepped barefoot into something nasty hidden in the long grass.

They got their good looks from their mother and one of the neighbours told Mari's mother that Mrs. Steadman had been crowned Miss Swansea East in 1961 and 1963.

On hot Saturday afternoons while Mari's mother was still on the bus coming home from town with the week's shop, Mrs. Steadman would be out in the garden in a pair of tennis-shorts and a bikini top mowing the lawn. As the sun began to sink Mr. Steadman would appear from the back of the house with a tray bearing iced drinks and the two of them would sit on the wooden bench in front of their French windows, sipping politely and smoking menthol cigarettes.

He was her second husband and so the two little girls were away every weekend with their other father who no one ever saw but everyone imagined must have been very handsome, but poor. Mari believed that Mrs. Steadman must still be in love with husband number one, because no one, especially not the beautiful

Mrs. Steadman could possibly love Mr. Steadman, who was a bank manager and was very bald and had a deformed right arm.

It was thought very odd that they should sit in the front of their house even though this was the place that got the sun in the afternoon and evening. Everyone knew that front gardens were just for show and not for sitting in where everyone could see you, but the Steadmans didn't seem to notice this. Nor did they mind that when they put the lights on in the evening everyone could see them sitting down to supper. They never seemed to draw their curtains, it was as if they were desperate to show that they had nothing to hide.

On week nights, if Mari had been sent to her room early, she would watch the Steadman family from her window. Sometimes they would all be in different rooms, all with the curtains wide open and the lights blazing. There was Mr. Steadman on the sofa in the sitting room reading a newspaper, while in the room next door, Barbara the eldest Steadman girl would be practising her piano. Upstairs in the master bedroom, Mrs. Steadman could be seen sitting at her dressing table brushing her long silky hair, while next door Bernadette seemed, from her bobbing head and lolloping gait, to be practising some dance steps. Mari could watch them go from room to room, and at moments like that, thought she knew more about them than they did about each other.

The Steadman girls never played in the street like the other children. They went to a private school and came home late bearing objects like a music case, or tennis rackets, or frothy tutus in big plastic bags. Their lives seemed very full and very mysterious to Mari, and she was never quite sure just who had got life right, all the other children with their gangs and games and the stifling ennui of long summer evenings when they were bored witless, or the Steadman girls with their elocution lessons, and tap dancing, and extra tuition. She used to feel sorry for them with all that endless schooling, until one day the Steadman girls had their picture in the paper and Mari's mother had sighed glumly and expressed the wish that Mari could have violin lessons. Mari had felt, when she heard this, that this lack of music classes was due to some failing on her part. When her father had chipped in gruffly that it would be a waste of time and money, this seemed to confirm for Mari that she, and all the other neighbourhood children, were beyond redemption. That they were scallywags, poor dabs, dirty *mochyn*s who would never get their photograph in the paper, unless it was for something bad. Like when June's brother Gareth had stolen a double decker bus while the driver was in a café, and ploughed up the bowling green in a vain attempt to make a daring getaway.

Mari thought that the Steadman girls would do wonderful things in the future. Maybe they'd be models or film stars, and would only come back to Wales to gloat and preen and show off their sports cars and their film star husbands. When Mari thought about this, she felt regret about not being their friend now. She thought that she ought to resent them, hate them even, but instead all she felt was a vivid, admiring longing. When the other kids at school shouted names at the girls and pranced about and said in a shriek "Oh, la-di-da. Lady muck!" Mari was impressed by the way the two girls held their heads up high and tossed their golden manes and didn't even blush. It was as if the insults and the name calling were having the opposite effect of the one intended. Instead of "bringing them down a peg or two" as June predicted, it only seemed to confirm their elite status on the street, and in the world beyond.

All that changed one day in July of 1969. Mari had just heard the surprising news that she, contrary to all expectation and hope, had passed her Eleven Plus. She would be going to the girls' grammar school and her father had promised her ten pounds to spend on anything she liked as a reward. She was upstairs in her bedroom making a long list of things she'd like when the doorbell rang. She ignored it and wrote "The Monkees L.P." then drew a picture of a record beside it. She was busy drawing concentric circles on the record and leaving some parts white to show that it was shiny, when the bell rang again more insistently. She heard the toilet flush, and then her mother shouting "For goodness sake, someone get the door." Dreamily Mari wandered out onto the landing and was halfway down the stairs when her mother rushed past her with the hem of her dress tucked into her knickers.

"Mum," she said, "Mum." But it was too late, her mother had flung open the door and was standing there with her flesh-coloured pantie girdle and suspenders and stockings and white puckery skin on show for all the world to see. Except that at that moment, she was thankfully facing the door, and so only Mari could see.

Mari went on down the stairs. She couldn't see who was at the door, but as she got closer, she heard a strange unfamiliar woman's voice. The voice was saying, or slurring rather, "Oh god, oh god, oh god, oh Jesus Christ." It sounded as if the voice was coming from underwater. It lurched and bubbled and choked and spluttered.

So far, Mari's mother had said nothing and Mari, sensing that something very unusual was about to happen, and still concerned about her mother's unfortunate state of undress in the region of her behind, went and stood alongside her at the door.

At first she didn't recognise Mrs. Steadman. Her face, besides being very pink and swollen and smeared with black trails of mascara, was contorted in a loose elastic way. One half of her hair was in big pink rollers while the other side looked matted and backcombed like a big blonde bird's nest. She didn't seem to notice Mari and took a deep gulp of air, then restarted her watery soliloquy, this time with a few more choice words beginning with "f" and "s" thrown in for good measure. When she spoke, Mari noticed, in the way one notices the smell of mown grass or perming lotion, that the air was filled with a smell like the smell of a dirty old man who'd once frightened her and June in the park. He'd smelled like that and sworn at them and when he started to unbutton his flies, she and June had run all the way home. It seemed right that all these things, the smell, and the swearing, and her mother's exposed rump, should all happen at the same time. It seemed to fit somehow.

Mari's mother finally spoke. Mari thought that she would surely tell Mrs. Steadman off for using such bad language, especially in front of the children, but she didn't. She spoke to her softly and said "Oh dear, oh dear. Whatever is the matter?" and Mari felt a pang of betrayal, because it was the voice her mother used with her when she had got stung by nettles or grazed her knee.

Mari's mother told Mrs. Steadman to come in, come in, she'd make a cup of tea. Mrs. Steadman lurched gratefully forward with something like a smile of thanks on her distorted face, caught her foot on the welcome mat and plunged forward heavily. Mari instinctively jumped back, while her mother clawed uselessly at the air as Mrs. Steadman hit the hall floor and lay there moaning. Mari's mother swung quickly into action. She had driven ambulances during the war, and now for the first time Mari could see some of the old fighting spirit come flooding back. She barked orders at Mari. "You take that arm. That's right. Now lift. Okay to your left. Hold her there, have you got her? Hang on."

They propped Mrs. Steadman against the cupboard under the stairs. Mari had to lean against her to keep her upright while her mother went to clear the passage into the best room. Mari watched her mother, as she moved chairs and pushed vases and other valuables out of harm's way. Mari noticed that somehow, in all the grappling with the very unsteady Mrs. Steadman, her mother's dress had unhitched itself from her underwear and she was restored to dignity, without the embarrassment of anyone telling her.

Mari's shoulder was pushed into the space between Mrs. Steadman's breasts while Mrs. Steadman's head lolled about and her eyes rolled up in their sockets. She was still moaning and Mari could feel her hot breath blasting the side of her face and smell the horrible smell. She didn't mind so much now, because at least this meant that Mrs. Steadman was still alive.

Mari's mother was talking now as if Mrs. Steadman wasn't there. "Drunk at this time in the afternoon," she said. "Hold her arm, that's it. Now watch the sideboard, to the settee, and let go. There!" Together, they threw Mrs. Steadman onto the leatherette sofa where she bounced in a loose rippling way.

"I'm going to make some strong black coffee. You watch her."

Mari stood solemnly regarding the heap on the sofa that was the elegant Mrs. Steadman. Her cheek was resting on one of the spiky pink rollers, but she didn't seem to mind. Mari wondered if she should adjust it somehow, take it out or put a pillow under her neck, but she had an idea that Mrs. Steadman might bite.

Mrs. Steadman was muttering something and waving her hand airily in Mari's direction. Mari's mother called out from the kitchen, "She's not going to be sick is she?" Mari crept closer and knelt down beside the settee.

"Pardon?" she said. Mrs. Steadman finally seemed to notice Mari. Her eyelids fluttered and her mouth twitched in a grimace that seemed a parody of a beauty queen's smile.

"You," she said, as she groped in vain to pat Mari's head, "you, my darling, can call me Irene, but don't tell them that." Then she began with the effing and blinding again and Mari drew back.

Mari's mother came in with the coffee and the two of them tried to sit Mrs. Steadman up, but she seemed fast asleep, even when Mari's mother shouted and slapped her face.

"We'll have to leave her, let her sleep it off," said Mari's mother sipping the black coffee as if she needed sobering up too, "God knows what's happened. Though really, there's no excuse. I don't know what your father's going to say."

They put a plastic bucket next to the slumbering Mrs. Steadman and tip-toed out, even though minutes before, they'd been shaking her and slapping her and screaming her name. Her mother had been saying "Penelope. Pen - el - oh - pee!" but to no avail. It was only when Mari said "Irene" that there was a flicker of any life. Her mother had looked at Mari oddly when she'd said the secret name, and so Mari had quickly said "Julie! Diane! Kathy! Rapunzel! Rumpelstiltskin!" and her mother had just shaken her head sadly and said, "I don't think that will work. She's completely blotto."

It was very strange that afternoon to be going about their business in the house while Mrs. Steadman lay drunk and snoring in the best room with the door wide open in case she threw up and choked. Her mother switched the radio off so that they could listen out for any suspicious noises and Mari stayed close by her mother's side in a way that she hadn't done for years. Her mother was busy making an apple tart, and Shepherd's Pie, and a chocolate sponge. She gave Mari the job of shelling the peas, and they took it in turns to go and look at Mrs. Steadman.

They were sitting at the formica-covered kitchen table playing Rummy and waiting for the cake to cool before they iced it, when Mrs. Steadman appeared at the door. She looked surprised to see them there. Her clothes were all rumpled, and she'd taken the curlers out of her hair. Her face looked very pale, except for where the plastic spokes of the curlers had been pressed into her cheek. She was swaying gently and holding onto the edge of the door to steady herself.

"Oh, God," she said, and Mari thought the awful string of bad language was going to pour forth again.

Mari's mother got to her feet and went and took Mrs. Steadman's hand and patted it gently.

"You'll want a shower," she said. Then as she led her up the stairs, she called back to Mari and told her to make some strong coffee.

Curiously, this was the first time that her mother had allowed Mari to use the kettle on her own without hovering about with morbid tales of scaldings and lifelong disfiguration. Mari felt a surge of pride as she poured the boiling water into the coffee pot without so much as a splash escaping. She even took it upon herself to open up the oven door and check that the tart wasn't burning. Upstairs she could hear the shower running and when it stopped she heard Mrs. Steadman crying and her mother's voice soothing and murmuring, saying "There now, you'll soon be right as rain. You can put this behind you and look to the future."

Mari tried to imagine what Mrs. Steadman was putting behind her, at first she had mistakenly thought it must be a towel. She could see it in her mind's eye, her mother passing the big yellow bath towel to a wet naked Mrs. Steadman and her explaining to her what to do with it. Then she corrected herself and the meaning of the phrase was clearer, though she still wished that she knew the whole story.

When they came downstairs, Mrs. Steadman was wearing the quilted nylon dressing gown that always hung on the back of the door in the bathroom, but no one ever wore.

Mari poured out the coffee and her mother handed it to Mrs. Steadman.

"Now you drink that and tell me what the trouble is, my dear. Perhaps I can help in some way?"

Mrs. Steadman looked uncertainly at her, then looked at Mari.

"Sometimes it helps to get things off your chest."

Mrs. Steadman sipped her coffee, then bit her lip. Mari thought she was going to confess to being in love with her first husband still. Her hands trembled as she replaced the cup in its saucer so that the china tinkled almost tunefully. Mari and her mother waited, finally Mrs. Steadman spoke.

"It's Geoff," she said, staring down at her hands as she washed them over each other, "he's been arrested."

She let that sink in, before she continued. "He's been arrested for taking money from the bank."

Mari pictured Mr. Steadman as one of the baddies in a cowboy film, he was wearing a Stetson and pulled a revolver from a holster that was slung around his waist. "Stick 'em up!" he said, with a gravelly voice that was not his own.

It was at that point in the conversation that Mari's mother

suggested she go upstairs and do her homework.

"I haven't got any!" Mari protested, but she recognized the tone in her mother's voice as one that would stand firm against any onslaught of opposition. It was the voice Mari heard almost every night before she went to bed. Reluctantly she trudged back up the stairs, then lay on her bed thinking about the events of the afternoon. She felt weary all of a sudden, and older. She hoped that her mother would tell her the whole story later and if she didn't maybe she could go over the road and talk to Mrs. Steadman herself. She'd say "Hello, Mrs. Steadman. Are you feeling better?" and Mrs. Steadman would say again "Oh, you can call me Irene."

Irene would confide in Mari. They'd talk woman to woman, and when the two girls came home, Irene would make them go to their rooms, while she poured Mari a cup of coffee and offered her chocolate cream eclairs.

Mari played out this conversation in her imagination again and again. She especially loved the part when Mrs. Steadman said "Call me Irene", and the bereft look on the daughters' faces when they were sent away from the intimate conversation she and their mother were having. They'd linger at the door staring hatefully at Mari as their mother said again, "You can call me Irene. Do have another eclair, my dear." And Mari would again say, "Don't mind if I do. Are these from Murray's, Irene?" and she'd reach for the proffered cake, the pastry as light as air, the chocolate cool and glossy and beaded with droplets of moisture, the cream inside heavy and thick and sweet. When Mari bit in, she knew she was tasting some forbidden fruit, the wages of sin perhaps, but at that moment it didn't matter. She took the cake again and again, and the first bite was always the sweetest.

Flock

This is a true story: one day when a woman was sitting on a train she noticed a flock of starlings and so, having nothing better to do, she watched them as they swooped and turned and changed shape from an arrow to a cloud to mere blob. Then a miracle happened. Or at least it felt like a miracle – the birds made a perfect heart-shape.

It was only for a moment, but the woman was sure it had happened; that it was a heart and furthermore, she had been meant to see it. Her only uncertainty was in regard to the meaning of this message.

The woman had never thought of herself as very attractive. She had managed to inherit all the worst characteristics and traits of her ancestors; the round face and domed forehead of her mother, the small eyes and tiny mouth of her father, her grandmother's heavy bovine chin. And she was short and thickset with a large bosom, which she tried to disguise by squeezing into undergarments that were three sizes too small.

She had never been kissed. At twenty-nine years of age she was as pure as the snow which falls through the broken roof of a deserted house and settles in the old porcelain bathtub to wait for spring.

But purity must surely be something that is chosen, not something that is thrust upon one. She would have been happy to be kissed; all she lacked was the opportunity.

It occurs to me that our visionary could have been a saint in the making were it not for the intervention that began with the actions of a young man called Geoffrey.

Ah, Geoffrey.

Geoffrey, Geoffrey, Geoffrey. Did not the name itself fly in on devil's wings?

Was it mere coincidence that in boarding the train he should choose carriage C and that the seat which he picked was the one opposite the heroine of our tale; the brooding, mysterious and unsullied Mary Williams?

And so the stage was set. Our players had taken their positions. Everything was ready.

Geoffrey, having sat down, had smiled absent-mindedly at Mary. Mary, colour rising in her cheeks, smiled back shyly. Geoffrey unbuttoned the jacket of his black suit, adjusted his shirt collar then drummed his fingers thoughtfully on the formica surface of the table that separated them. Mary smoothed her skirt then rested her hands on the table with her fingers tightly interlaced as if she were praying.

Actually she *was* praying. She frowned, as she concentrated hard and addressed the god that lived in her head. "Oh, please, please, let me think of something to say. Let me talk sensibly. Let me be interesting, make him listen. Make him notice me."

Geoffrey *had* noticed her. He looked at her as she studied her hands. He noticed her mouth, which was a delicate rosebud, and her cheeks, which were unfashionably plump and healthy. She looked like a country girl from a Hogarth print. Geoffrey assumed that she was married – that she had a brood of fat children, was milky and soft and comforting, and when her husband came to her at night he tumbled into the flesh of their shared bed without fireworks or histrionics, but with a pleasure that was muffled and dumplingy.

Thinking about this made our hero a little hot under the collar. Oh, for an old fashioned train, he thought, the sort where you could actually open the window; the sort with compartments and net luggage racks and faded posters that advertised Skegness and Weston-super-Mare and Great Yarmouth. Oh, for the long ago past; the promenade and tartan slippers and naughty postcards and one piece swim-wear and cottage pie and billowing steam trains and hot glutinous tapioca pudding. He laid his hands, damp palms down, on the cool of the table and the furthest tips of his fingers touched Mary's warm knuckles.

And there it was. The sudden electric charge of human flesh. He pulled his hands back as if stung. Said, "Oh. Sorry." Looked into her eyes, which, though they were small, were so very brown that they looked black. The lashes were thick and long and accentuated the brightness of the eyes. They were extremely pretty eyes, he thought.

She mumbled something in reply to his apology which he did not understand, but he read the smile; the quick dance of the eyes, the briefest lifting of the brows, then the coy lowering of the lids.

"Pardon?" said Geoffrey.

Mary looked flustered, murmured a little string of tiny words: "Pardon, oh, um, sorry, that's all right."

Geoffrey loosened his tie and undid the top button of his shirt and stretched and twisted his neck.

"Phew," he sighed, "it's very close."

"Close?" said Mary. For a moment the term made no sense, then she remembered. "Yes. It's warm."

"For the time of year…" continued Geoffrey.

"Yes, very close for the time…"

"…for the season."

And then she was lost for words. She picked up her paperback meaning to fan her face, but it was too cumbersome to waft and with one flick of the wrist she threw it straight into Geoffrey's lap.

Just at the moment when Geoffrey gave a muffled "Ooof" the train slowed and pulled into Cardiff. Mary, mortified by this accidental act of seeming aggression was too horrified to apologize. Instead she gasped, she fluttered. Geoffrey having seen and understood completely how the book came to land painfully on his inner thigh, soothed her with a smiling "That's all right" and picked the book up.

With eyes that shone under half lowered lids, Mary had smiled back.

Geoffrey turned the book over and studied the cover.

"Ah, *The Novels of Jane Austen*," he'd said pleasantly. "Which one are you reading at the moment?"

Before Mary had a chance to speak, a large Adidas bag landed with a thud on the table between our lovers.

Enter the prince of darkness and his sulphurous egg sandwiches and his armpits tainted with last night's vindaloo and his breath kissed by two very recent swift pints of real ale. He huffed, he puffed. He took a newspaper from his bag and tossed it onto the seat beside Mary. He peeled off his olive jacket and flung that carelessly onto the seat next to Geoffrey. He extracted the aforementioned eggy delicacies from his sports bag, along with an out-sized can of Coke, two packets of cheese and onion crisps and a large saveloy. Then, casting his eyes over the two occupants of the table he proclaimed "Alright?" and flashed a perfect set of teeth framed by two charming dimples. Then he zipped up his bag and heaved it onto the rack above, scratched himself abundantly, stretched, and then, with all the subtlety of a baboon, he adjusted the elastic of his underpants. He dropped heavily and comfortably onto the seat beside Mary, bouncing her unpleasantly and neatly displacing her elbow from the arm rest as he did so.

With one tentative finger Geoffrey slid the copy of Jane Austen across the table towards Mary. Mary opened her mouth; she was about to say *Persuasion* when another voice filled the hesitating void.

"What you reckon to Tottenham, then?"

Geoffrey, sitting up to attention, looked quizzically at the man. Mary noticed how pale and astonished Geoffrey looked suddenly.

"Reckon they'll give Man United a run for their money?"

"Sorry?" said Geoffrey.

"Ah," said the stranger and he pointed his rolled up newspaper at Geoffrey in a threatening way. Geoffrey visibly shrank.

"You a rugby man, eh?" the stranger waggled the paper. "Triple Crown this year mate. Eh? Remember J.P.R.? What year was that? '77? '78? Barry John? King John. Aaah." He groaned, then slapped his paper down on the table. "The three feathers, eh?" and he punched his chest heartily. "Wear them with pride. What you reckon?"

"Erm…" said Geoffrey at last.

The man offered his palms to Geoffrey in theatrical protest, "Don't say it. I knows what you going to say. The way I sees it, you got to believe, see. Huh? It's like that Tinkerbelle init? You don't say you don't believe in fairies, though I've met a few in my time." He laughs here: arf, arf, arf. "Same with Wales init? Never say die. Never say die."

Wisely, Geoffrey did not say die, or anything else for that matter, but smiled a weak, crooked smile with his eyebrows still knitted into a frown.

The man satisfied that a conversation had taken place, smiled and sighed and shook his head, then he craned his head around to take a good long look at Mary. His eyes grazed her bosom.

"And what about the missus eh? You follow the rugby, love?"

"No. I…" despite the warm glow that being mistaken for Geoffrey's wife had given her; the little blush-inducing thrill, she was about to say that she was not "the missus", but her reply was swept away on a tide of further cozy banter. She looked at Geoffrey. Geoffrey looked at her and raised his eyebrows. The corners of his mouth quirked up briefly and his shoulders shifted in the merest hint of a shrug. Mary smiled and while she was still smiling Geoffrey stood up, straightened his jacket and tie, brushed himself off, picked up his briefcase and muttered something that sounded like "mmthinkumgotothebuffetcarsoon" and was gone before Mary had a chance to register what was happening.

The stranger beside her opened his plastic bag of sandwiches and began to munch and slurp loudly. Mary picked up her book and read the same sentence over and over, but it failed to register in any way. With the book held open before her, she slipped her eyes sideways to take in the stranger. His face was turned away from her, though she could see his cheek busily working at the food. His ear too, went up and down with his jaw movements. This struck Mary as comical so she laughed, then remembering herself, she stared at her book, pointing one finger at the text as though to illustrate the fact that this was what had made her laugh.

She was aware that the stranger had turned to look at her. She composed herself. He turned away again. She glanced at her watch, then up the aisle where Geoffrey had disappeared – where she expected to see his return. She was certain that he would bring her a cup of coffee or tea too. Why was she certain? This cannot be answered, though perhaps the birds and Geoffrey's gentle smile had something to do with it.

She rehearsed her surprise (though of course she wouldn't be surprised) ready for when he arrived with two drinks. "For me? Oh really? You shouldn't have. Oh, thank you, you're a gentleman." As she imagined this she was smiling foolishly to herself and all but mouthing the words.

But he was very slow in returning, there must have been a queue. There was often a very long queue. People didn't just have sandwiches anymore. No, they had microwaved burgers and warmed up bacon and eggs and hot toasted sandwiches and gin and tonic and goodness knows what else.

It struck Mary, as she found her eyes focused on the young girl at the adjacent table who was carefully peeling back the lid from a tall white polystyrene cup and releasing its faint breath of steam, that this girl had left for the buffet after Geoffrey. And look, now she was already back.

Of course, the young girl was pretty. Was showing too

much leg and far too much cleavage. She'd probably jumped the queue, while the men, half of them from lust and half from politeness, had let her. Mary knew which category Geoffrey fell into – so he'd still be waiting in a well-mannered fashion, but not for long now.

Next to her the stranger had dispatched the sandwiches and was feeding the saveloy into his mouth with greasy fingers, like a sword swallower. Then he opened his crisps, took a handful, stuffed them into his mouth while Mary listened (had she any choice?) as his molars worked on them loudly.

She stared at her page with eyes that grew a little glazed. The train, between dull swishing noises, gave off a long drawn-out two-tone donkey bellow. Mary's eyes were almost closed when an open packet of crisps was thrust in front of her. The sudden oniony smell shot to her senses like a sniff of smelling salts.

"Crisp?" the stranger asked.

To be polite, Mary took a crisp that was no bigger than her thumbnail and popped it onto her tongue where it dissolved tastelessly.

"Your old fella's taking his time i'n he?"

"Um…"

"I'd give him gyp if I was you when he shows up – leaving you on your tod like this."

Mary had said nothing, but felt unreasonably angry with Geoffrey for deserting her. She pictured herself and Geoffrey in an old fashioned dining room. There was an arched oak clock on the tiled fireplace and a bevelled mirror hanging on a silver chain over a sideboard. The table was lain with a white cloth embroidered with ladies in bell-shaped crinolines, and on it was bone handled cutlery and a rosebud tea set, and in the centre was a large plate of bread and butter. In a corner, on a glass fronted bookcase was a Bakelite radio tuned to the home service. Mary would be standing and Geoffrey would be sitting at the table and she would say to him rather firmly, her mouth set in a straight line while she unknotted her frilly apron and folded it, she would say "Geoffrey, you left me alone and quite defenceless on the train today." And he would say "My darling" or "Sweetheart, I was a heartless brute" and beg her forgiveness.

The room she imagined was a real one and belonged to her grandparents. The apron she wore was the one her grandmother wore every Sunday.

The train drew into Newport. The young girl with too much cleavage rose, shrugged on a tattered leather jacket and reached for her rucksack on the rack. The stranger put down his crisps and was on his feet and helping the young girl to reach her bag in a twinkling. She thanked him and was gone. He sat down again and glanced at his watch, then turned to Mary.

"He's a long time, love. He's not ill or nothing is he? Mate of mine's diabetic – flakes out at the drop of a hat, want me to go and look for him?"

Mary, touched by his consideration and momentarily alarmed – that yes, perhaps Geoffrey had collapsed and was lying helpless somewhere, said "Thank you, that's all right, but I'll go, if you'll excuse me."

The stranger once again put down his packet of cheese and onion and stood up to let Mary out. When she reached for her bag and coat, he said "No, no, you leave them here, they'll be safe enough with me."

Mary began the long journey up the train to the buffet, her heart pounding with fear. However, no sooner had she passed into the very next carriage, than who should she find but Geoffrey. He was sitting very comfortably, jacket and tie dispensed with, chatting animatedly and amiably with a sophisticated lady, who, Mary decided, was wearing too much make up.

Mary stopped when she saw him and stood in the aisle close by, uncertain whether to breeze on past to the buffet, or return the way she had come. Geoffrey looked up at her. At first he looked blank, then recognition dawned on him and expressed itself in widened eyes. He looked guilty. Guilty as hell.

Mary turned on her heel and rushed back towards the

sanctuary of her seat. She felt heartbroken, betrayed and foolish. Oh, so foolish. She began to cry. Emotion tugged at the corners of her mouth, dragging it down in a grimace of agony. The train lurched forward and she stumbled blindly, barely suppressing a great ruptured sob.

The stranger had seen her and was on his feet, braced for action. As Mary reached him he grasped her shoulders in a way that Mary had only ever dreamed of being held.

"What's up love? Did you find him? Is he ill?"

Mary lifted her pink, tear-streaked face to him and said "He's through there," between sobs.

The stranger said "Come on, quick."

And Mary said "No, no... it's... he's..." while her fingers clutched the sleeve of his jumper.

The stranger, straining to free from her hummingbird touch and hungry to prove himself, said "What? What?"

"He's..." she said dramatically between choking noises, "he's not ill... he's... with a woman."

Well, it's hard to express exactly what you mean between sobs. Short words and phrases are all that can be fitted into the narrow crevices between hiccuping gasps. And heroes, when they're on the brink of action, when the wilting maiden is collapsing like a punctured ball in their primed and hungry arms, when the adrenaline is pumping through their delicious and clot-free veins and their quick minds are trained and pulsing with a fast response: when all that is happening, well, they don't wait for long and elaborate explanations.

"The bastard!" the stranger declared in a bellow and he lifted Mary bodily to one side. Mary, breathless and half-faint from excitement, swooned as the stranger charged up the aisle looking broader and taller and more bull-like with every stride.

In the next carriage, the stranger saw the same tableau that Mary had witnessed. The stranger, like Mary, stood still and Geoffrey, noticing the figure hovering to his left, looked up mildly and dispassionately. Then he registered recognition once again.

Geoffrey was about to nod politely (well, dismissively actually) and return to the nice chat he'd been having with the rather attractive lady who was a P.A. at the BBC and had recently broken off her engagement, when this chap; this nasty, rough, brutish chap shouted: "YOU BASTARD!" and having yanked Geoffrey out of his seat by his collar and tie to impart the message at close range, had punched him squarely on the jaw which sent him straight back, in a crumpled heap, to his seat again. Then, having informed Geoffrey that he didn't deserve her and having given the P.A. from the BBC a look of withering contempt, the stranger was gone.

Somewhere in the vast brooding heavens between Newport and Cardiff, a flock of starlings congratulated each other on their work and spiralled upwards in a neat funnel shape. One bird, who was known to be something of a ring leader, hung below the flock, tipping and lifting its wings. When viewed from the Inter City 125 this formation looked astonishingly like an exclamation mark. Sadly not a single person noticed.

Running Away
with the Hairdresser

The sun was shining that day, although there was also enough of a
fresh breeze to send clouds skimming and chasing across the
impossibly blue sky. At the top of Pen Brân we had watched the
shadows of those clouds darken by turns the far hills and fields.
Then, in those fleeting shadows, I detected nothing threatening;
no hint of the trouble to come.

In the valley below us, running by the side of the river was
the railway and on the tracks, hurtling eastward towards England,
was a train. I watched it, I remember, full of longing. I wanted to
escape even as I lay on the scrub grass of a Welsh mountainside
with the girl I believed I loved in my arms. The girl who, I
thought, loved me, but instead of settling in the stillness of the
moment, I was yearning for movement; for freedom, for the
clouds' wild rampage away from the slumbering world.

She was married, and had a son. She'd brought him along
that day. He was a pathetic scrap: six years old, lisping, stick-thin,
freckled, and with hair so white and eyes such a watery blue you'd
have thought him an albino. He clung to her incessantly as if the
wind might blow her away, and maybe he was right to detect the
threat of some ancient and elemental force which plucked at her,
and called her from their little home above the hairdressing shop,
away from the town, the valley, and Wales, and into the dark
underworld of England and beyond.

When she spoke to her son she called him, not by his name,

but "boy", as women in those parts often do. The boy was sulking and complaining of a headache, and whenever he said it, his eyes slid towards me accusingly, as though I were its chief cause.

"Come on, boy," she said, sounding and looking more like a big sister than his mother, "I'll race you to the top."

But he grizzled all the more, like the bony bag of misery he was. I didn't help matters much, I'll admit. I resented the sudden appearance of this mawkish creature, the restrictions he put on what we did during our brief time together. The watering down of our pleasures, the whispered words, the way she untangled my hand from hers whenever the kid was within a hundred yards.

We had precious little time together anyway, what with that hunkering, suspicious, ex-army husband of hers, and the hairdressing business with its rows of blue-rinsed old bags lined up beneath the dryers like over-grown turkeys under a grill; all gizzard-neck and gobble-gobble, and bulging, rolling eyes always on the look out for something to peck to death.

She was just twenty-two and only looked sixteen if she looked a day. I was thirty-eight, and a born liar. I told her I was twenty-nine, thus placing myself in the same decade as her. She never guessed the truth. I had never married, and secretly, I had decided that I was never going to get tied down like that. If she assumed otherwise, well then, that was her problem.

I still smoked back then, which is yet another clue to my state of mind – even at almost forty I thought that I was going to live forever.

All of her energy was going into entertaining the boy. They were careening over the hill, plucking daisies and making long chains and winding themselves up in them. I lay back on my elbows, with ankles crossed and a Players Number 6 stuck in the corner of my mouth, squinting at the sun and letting the frown stay creased between my brows even when the sun went in.

"You're sulking aren't you?"

She was standing over me, I remember, and the sun gaped blindingly over her left shoulder. The boy had wandered off in search of bigger daisies. She kicked at the sole of my shoe, "You're bloody jealous of 'im aren't you?"

"Grow up!" I said in a low voice. "Get a grip, for christsake."

She pulled a face, then turned to check on the kid's whereabouts. I took my chance and launched myself at her ankles, and grappled her down. We'd messed around like this before, giggling and tickling one another and play-wrestling, and I was laughing, except that I could detect a hollow edge to the sound. And she wasn't laughing at all.

It was in those seconds that all our dreams began to crack and distort at the edges. I was still laughing my hollow laugh, still caught in the pretext of affectionate play, when her elbow smashed into my nose; hard enough to stun me and hard enough to produce a few droplets of thin snotty blood.

'Bitch!' I snarled, and a few other things besides. I rolled away from her, and blinked and snorted like a scolded dog who's been whacked on the snout with a newspaper.

She was up and running, and for once, calling the boy's name. "Hugh!" she yelled. "Hugh!" over and over, until it no longer sounded like a name or a word you would recognize, but some she-animal's mating call.

We both heard the splash. It was sudden and it was out of place; there was no water nearby that we could see, and for all those reasons and more it was frightening.

Her cries now took on an even more breathless and distorted quality as she raced toward the sound, with me at her heels. We got there while ripples of black water were still making hypnotic circles around the space where the boy had fallen in. You could see how the land had collapsed in on itself, how years of earth and grass had knotted themselves together into a conspiracy that hid the empty air of an old mine shaft and the underground pool it led to. I stood there marvelling at it, noting the fringed grass at its edges and the lace-like display of roots that were so diagrammatically exposed and the cold air that seemed to rise up from the water.

Then, rousing me at last from my reverie, I saw from the corner of my eye that she was taking off her shoes and socks, shaking off her jacket.

"You can't swim," I said, kicking off my shoes, and for a second we were both tearing at our clothes like hungry lovers in some passionate race against time. I won the race, and bare feet first, I was swallowed by first the air, and then the water. I went down fast, blind and shocked into the engulfing cold, then came up for air, and then went under again with eyes open at the stinging dark, and precious little time in my lying poisoned lungs.

I couldn't find him. I came up again, gasping and treading water and not even daring to look up to where she stood. The third time I went under seemed the longest. I went down as far as I dared, but found nothing solid there, no silty bed or rocks or debris and no half-drowned boy either.

My mind, however, was playing tricks with me. Perhaps it was the shock or the fear or the cold that caused it, whatever it was doesn't matter actually; all I know is that while I swam around down there I suddenly felt very calm. Happy, almost. And I thought about three things. The first was a song, which I suppose, I seemed to hear rather than actually think about in any concrete way. It was playing in my head like a film soundtrack. It was The Spencer Davies Group's "Keep on Running" and the words seemed to me like directions for that very instance in my life, "Keep on running," they sang, "keep on hiding".

At the same time I had a sort of vision of myself running down the high street in the sunshine, and she was running with me; she was by my side holding my hand and we didn't care who saw us, or who knew about us, or anyone or anything, because we were gone, and out of there and never coming back. But as I swam and ran and my lungs grew tighter and more desperate for air, I lost my grip on her hand. Growing weak, my hand was spasmodically pumping the watery nothingness in search of her lost dream hand when it finally found the thin half-dead reality of his.

It should have been a moment of triumph; of relief, of heroism, of everything that is good and sweet and noble, but instead of that, one evil and corrupting idea leapt on me like a water serpent in the deep. The idea was that I should leave him there, that he was dead already and I needed to save myself. It was a tragic accident and I had done all I could, and I could not be blamed, and she would be free, we would be free. And I saw the boy's life stretching into the future and deemed it a sickly sad future, not worth living.

It is not a memory I am proud of. I could blame all kinds of temporary madness brought on by the lack of oxygen. I might even conjure up some evil supernatural force infecting my mind, a jealous ghost, a spiteful water baby, alien forces of destruction, but these would only be vague excuses, a thin veneer of lies which could do nothing to save me, or salve the wounds of terrible self knowledge. And the truth was I wanted him dead. Not just because I felt that his death would free us, but also because, like some ancient jealous God I wanted to destroy him and thus weaken her.

Then I felt a movement from the boy and without thought, I found myself swimming, swimming upwards, with him hooked under one arm and the daylight like the phosphorescence from an angel's wing calling us home, and back to the world.

I have told no-one of this. Instead I have spent the best part of sixteen years running. But I ran away alone, the vision I had had of the two of us was only that: a vision as illusory as a dream or a human form glimpsed in a cloud. The running away does not make me free however much I like to think it does. The running away is my curse, my punishment for darker sins, even if they were never quite acted on. Those sins may have been left there in Wales, in a dark gash in the hill's surface, in the ripples of a secret pool; the soul's foot caught forever in the weeds.

Too Perfect

The man and the woman were standing side by side at the marina, studying the new housing development on the other side of the water. He had been expressing surprise tinged with disgust at the sight of the red brick buildings with their gabled windows and arches and as he put it "post modern gee-gaws". While she, having no knowledge of what had stood there before and no great opinion on architecture, said nothing.

Then into the silence that hovered between them he suddenly offered "Do you mind?" and before he had finished asking, took her hand in his. In reply she gave a squeeze of assent, noting as she did how large and warm and smooth his hand was.

To a passerby it would have looked like nothing out of the ordinary. He or she, on seeing this man and woman by the water's edge, would assume that this hand-holding was a commonplace event for them. But it wasn't. This was the first, the only time of any real physical contact between them.

Later, still awkwardly holding hands, each now afraid that letting go might signal some end to that which had not yet even begun, they made their way to the old Town Hall, once the home of commerce and council and now a centre for literature. This was the purpose of their trip, the reason why at seven that morning, she had stood at the window of her bedsit in Cambrian Street, Aberystwyth, waiting for the tin-soldier red of his Citroen to emerge around the corner.

Each had expressed an interest in visiting the Centre and had behaved as if they were the only two people in the world with such a desire. That was why, uncharacteristically, he hadn't suggested the trip to the other members of his tutorial group. It was also the reason why Claire had omitted to tell any of her friends, why she had agreed to wake Ginny that morning at ten o'clock, despite the fact that she and Dr. Terrence Stevenson would probably be enjoying coffee and toast together in Swansea by then.

Terry, as he was known to colleagues and students alike, was a large man, over six feet, with large bones and large appetites, which now as he neared fifty expressed itself in his frame. He had once been lithe and muscular but his body had thickened with age. He blamed too many years at a desk, the expansion of his mind at the expense of an expanding behind. But he dressed well enough, choosing dark tailored jackets and corduroy or chino slacks, as well as the odd devilish tie, which was about as subversive as he got. In colder weather, as on this grey October day, he wore his favourite black Abercrombie overcoat of cashmere and wool mix. The coat hung well from the shoulders and had the effect of tapering his body, disguising its imperfections with a veneer of powerful authority and masculinity.

Claire thought he looked like one of the Kray twins in this coat of his, and to her that signalled a sort of dangerous sexuality. She could not help but imagine herself engulfed in that coat, held willing captive in its soft folds.

Next to him, she looked tiny, even less than her five feet and a half inch. Claire had very long hair, grown in excess to compensate perhaps for her lack of height. It hung down, straight and sleek to her bottom and a great deal of her time was taken up with this hair: washing, combing and plaiting it before she went to bed each night. Most of the time she wore it loose and her gestures, the movement of her head, body and hands were all done in such a way as to accommodate her river of hair. When eating, for example, she would hold the fork in one hand while with the other she held her hair away from the plate. She was very proud of her hair and if asked which part of herself she liked the most, that would be what she would choose. Her last boyfriend, whom she had met at the Fresher's Dance at college and dated for almost three years, had loved her hair; had sometimes spread it over her naked body, Lady Godiva style when they made love; had once even made the pretence of tying himself to her by it.

Claire's body was like a boy's: flat chested and slim hipped. And today she was dressed like a boy too, with jeans and heavy black lace-up boots and a white shirt and a man's tweed jacket two sizes too big. Through both her right eyebrow and right nostril she wore tiny silver rings and her eyes and lips were exaggerated with make up in shades of reddish brown. She seldom smiled, but when she did her entire face was transformed into something not quite wholly beautiful, but something very like it.

They had trudged through an exhibition of artifacts relating to the town's one famous poet: the scribbled postcards, the crumpled snapshots, the yellowing newspaper clippings, all framed for posterity like the relics of some dead saint. Terry had begun by clucking and tutting yet more disapproval of the venture, disapproval he'd been nurturing and planning since he first heard of it, but with Claire by his side he found himself softening, growing acclimatised to her open-minded acceptance of all such endeavours.

They spoke in whispers, though the place was almost entirely deserted, this being after all a grey Tuesday in October, and around the back, beneath some engravings by Peter Blake they kissed their first kiss. It did not feel like the world's best kiss for either of them, but did well enough as an awkward, uncertain snatched preliminary to better things. Afterwards Claire had wanted to wipe her mouth with the back of her hand, not from disgust but just because the kiss was a little wet. His mouth had swallowed hers, had not measured out the size of her lips yet.

After the kiss they each felt like a conspirator in some deadly plot; what they would create that day felt as if it might be as deadly as Guy Fawkes' gunpowder, as bloody as any revolution.

The second kiss came as they sat in a deserted bar of the

Pump House. The barman, a student, they decided, was propped against the far end of the counter, his head bent over a book. They took turns to guess what the book might be. Terry said it was a handbook about computing, and she thought it was a script of something like *Reservoir Dogs*.

The clock above the bar, a faux-nautical affair, hung with nets and cork floats and plastic lobster and crab, read twelve-fifteen. They had the afternoon and the early evening to spend together. He was thinking about the Gower coast, a cliff walk, the lonely scream of wheeling gulls and the sea a grey squall bubbling under the wind. She was thinking about a hotel room, the luggage-less afternoon ascent in the lift to the en-suite room and the champagne, herself languishing on the sheets, feeling intolerably beautiful under his grateful gaze.

After that second kiss, which was prolonged, they wrenched themselves away and began to speak in a strange language of unfinished sentences and hesitant murmurings.

"Oh."

"Gosh."

"You know we…"

"I never…"

"Oh my…"

"We shouldn't…"

"I never thought…"

"Nor me…"

"I mean, I always thought that maybe…"

"Me too…."

Then they kissed again and the barman, who wasn't a student, raising his eyes briefly from his novel by Gorky, watched them with mild interest and thought they made an odd pair.

The odd pair finished their drinks: pints of real ale. She stubbed out her cigarette and they made their way towards the exit, his arm thrown protectively around her shoulders while his broad back wore her tiny arm, its fingers clutching the cloth, like a curious half belt.

The sky looked by now greyer and darker than before. To the West a blue-black curtain advanced, promising heavy rain and a wind blew up from the East, sending her hair on a frantic aerial dance. They ran across the empty square as raindrops as big as shillings began marking the paving stones with dark circles.

Then she half stumbled and he caught her and in catching her, gathered her to him and they kissed a fourth time, this the best, with the rain splashing their heads and water pouring down their faces.

When they had done with this, this their unspoken moment of willingness and promise and wilfulness, their pact to indulge in what they knew was an unwise thing, he quickly kissed the tip of her nose and then hand in hand they began to run again.

Under the covered walkway, they slowed down and shaking off the worst of the rain from their hair and clothes, barely noticed a man standing close by. He was busy putting away a tripod and Terry muttered, "Afternoon" and the man, grinning broadly replied, "Thanks".

Naturally neither of them made much of this, assuming it to be yet another curious aspect of Welshness. A further example of the strange smiling politeness, the thanking of bus drivers and so on, the chatting to strangers which each of them had at first perceived as alien, but now despite their breeding, accepted and in part adopted.

Later that afternoon, in his car near a field in the north of Gower, with the day as dark as ever they almost made love. The next day, back in Aberystwyth, they did make love.

She had rung him from the payphone in the hall of her house when she was certain all the other students had gone out. His wife had answered the phone and she'd given her the prearranged message, which was that she'd "found the journal with the Lawrence article he'd wanted."

What happened that Wednesday was perhaps rather sad, though not necessarily inevitable. It became clear to both of them that what they sought was a fugitive moment; that there could be no more than this, the furtive opening of the front door, the climbing of the stairs, the single bed dishevelled and cramped under the sloping roof, his glances at his watch, her ears constantly straining for any sounds from down below. Both of them too tense for pleasure, but going through its rigours, him professionally, she dramatically.

Afterwards, when they had dressed again, they sat side by side on the bed like strangers in a doctor's waiting room, each thinking silently about how to end it, how to escape. She took his hand and held it on her lap, then began to speak.

"Your wife…"

"Catherine?"

"She sounded…"

"Yes."

"She sounded…"

"Nice?"

"She is. I…"

"I don't…"

"I can't…"

"I think that…"

"Me too.'

He sighed. She understood his sigh to mean that he didn't want to leave and she sighed back at the thought that he might cancel his three o'clock lecture in order to stay. He had sighed because he was wondering how long he ought to stay to make it seem at least remotely respectable. He rested his eyes on the small wooden bookcase next to her bed. She had all the required texts as well as a rather unhealthy number of books by and about the American poet Sylvia Plath. This made him sigh again. She was trying very hard to imagine him back in his study, with the coffee cups on the window ledge and the view of the National Library and the letter trays overflowing with student essays and she sighed again because now that she'd seen him in his underwear that ordinary idea seemed impossible.

He stood suddenly, ready to go, but somehow his watch

had become entangled with her hair and she gave a yelp of pain as he unthinkingly yanked at it, ripping the hair from her head. They both looked aghast at the tangled clumps sprouting from the metal bracelet of his watch. He pulled at them but they cut into his fingers and stretched and curled and slipped and clung until finally they snapped, leaving short tufts poking out here and there.

Tears had come to her eyes with the sudden pain. He looked at her and seeing this, with ill-disguised irritation as much at himself as with her, said "I'm sorry," then bluntly, "Why don't you get that cut?"

That would have been the end of the story, except that some moments, elusive as they may seem when lived, come back in other guises, unbidden. Theirs was a photograph, unfortunately a very good photograph of a young girl on tip toes, her long wet hair lifted wildly in the wind and a black-coated man bent over her, his hands delicately cupping her upturned face as their lips met. Rain glistened on their faces and shone in silvery puddles on the paving stones at their feet and behind them the sky was a black brooding mass of cloud.

It was a timeless image, a classic to be reproduced over and over, whose currency was love, truth and beauty. The people who bought the poster and the stationery range and the postcard assumed that it must have been posed, that it was really too perfect.

Tongue

Lately, if there was one thing to keep Paul awake at night it was this; thoughts of his tongue. Or more precisely thoughts about the position of his tongue in his mouth as he lay in bed with his head on the pillow hoping for sleep. He might be dog tired or dead drunk, but if that one discomforting thought about where to put his tongue came into his head, then he was sunk.

Paul, as it happened, had many better reasons to lay awake at night worrying. He could, for example worry about money, or about his future. He could toss and turn about the meaning of life. He could fret about the existence of God or aliens, or about wars past, present and future.

Alternatively, and more productively, he could lie awake plotting new sculptures or thinking up ways to integrate a sort of self awareness into his art; a translatable message to the planet. But no, all he thought about was his tongue.

It was in the morning, as he waited for the kettle to boil and poured milk over his cornflakes, when he thought about these greater problems. Then he'd shuffle off in the track-suit bottoms he'd slept in, to the studio where he made his sculptures. He'd review the previous day's work, run his eye over their mutant forms and gear himself up to another day by trying to focus on the problems of construction and aesthetics, rather than the trying problem of what he was going to do with all those sculptures. Just as at night he avoided all thoughts of his tongue and invariably ended up thinking of just that, so by day he tried not to think about what to do with his sculptures when they were finished. And the thing that he really mustn't do, was to wonder what the point was. That was deadly.

He made his sculptures from scrap metal which he collected from the town's dump, or from scrap yards, or from the skips that people so thoughtfully left planted on the pavements outside their houses. This, he felt, meant his work was environmentally friendly and pure; politically correct – a comment, in fact, on the consumer society. The problem however, was, were these things; these painstaking constructions of his, worthwhile? Or were they just junk in a different shape? Junk resembling zoological forms. Junk as myth. Junk as politics. Or junk as junk?

Increasingly pursued by these ghosts of doubt, perhaps because of what his new girlfriend Karen had recently said to him, he was feeling more than a little depressed. This seemed unfair as actually he'd thought that having a girlfriend, especially one as pretty as Karen, would have cheered him up.

And it had cheered him up at first. He'd felt himself softening at the edges and melting into the world. He was no longer alone. It had taken weeks for Karen to insinuate herself into his life. It had been three weeks before he'd even let her come to his house, and then a whole month before he'd let her see the studio.

They'd been seeing each other for exactly ten weeks when he took her to his studio. The house he lived in backed onto a tiny deserted chapel. The front of the building was carefully bricked up, but the back door, he discovered, was actually hidden in the wall, behind the overgrown weeds at the bottom of his garden and no one had bothered to board this up, let alone lock it. By degrees he'd liberated this place from its original purpose and made it his own little shrine to art.

"Come with me," he'd said to Karen one morning. "I want to lead you up the garden path." He'd pulled her along by the hand through the dew soaked grasses.

"Oh. Kinky," she'd said, letting herself trail limply after him.

He opened the door and giggling, she entered.

He'd watched her as she wandered here and there in that stately way of hers with her hands clasped behind her back. She wove her way between the four foot-tall pig made of cogs, wheels, bedsprings, frying pans and exhaust pipe. Past the tin can sheep, the wire mermaid, Eve and the Serpent; the sketches strewn on the floor and thumb-tacked to the walls; the welding equipment, the soldering iron, and the mound of rusty scrap which Paul tended to eye in much the same way, he thought, that Michelangelo must have once eyed a good piece of marble.

This was a big step, letting her see all this. It was not quite a privilege, but it was certainly a sign of her importance in his life. Letting her into the studio was, Paul thought, a bit like saying "I love you."

So he stood watching her as she gazed around and all his work seemed to suddenly take on a golden glow bathed in the light of her eyes, and then she turned to him and said, "Don't you ever think it's just silly sometimes?"

Karen's hair was long and golden blonde and she'd recently had it permed into tumbling Pre-Raphaelite curls. She was wearing a tight T-shirt that had the word "Angel" printed over her chest. He could make out the faint outline of her bra; the straps and the ridges of seam underneath. The back of this T-shirt, he knew, had the word "Bitch" printed on it. This had puzzled him when she'd first worn it. Why have such things splashed across your body? Didn't women hate labels like that anyway? Increasingly, as he noticed more and more young women sporting these tops, it had begun to irritate him. Why "Angel"? Why "Bitch"? The two were unrelated; it should have said "Angel" and "Devil". Or "Bitch" and "Dog".

Looking at her, he found himself remembering how he used to be smug about being young. How ridiculous, he considered, to be smug about something like that; something so transient and accidental. He remembered a saying about "youth being wasted on the young". How true, he thought, how very true.

Karen was looking at him, her eyebrows raised expectantly, quizzically, innocently. He blinked at her. The smile she wore, which was probably just the same as the smile he'd fallen in love with, seemed twisted ironically at the edges; seemed to see through not only him, but the whole brittle carapace of civilization; seemed to mock him.

"Don't you think it's just silly?"

The trouble was that as soon as she'd said it, it did seem silly. No, not just silly, but downright stupid. Not to mention egotistical and pointless.

"Hmmm," he said and resisted stroking his chin.

"I mean..." she said, pausing while she rested her hand comfortably on the pig's neck, "don't get me wrong – it is nice. It's a marvellous hobby to have, and I couldn't do it, but well... you know what I mean."

He winced at the words "nice" and "hobby" and his neck bristled. Karen turned away and peered at the figure of Eve, which had a beer-can serpent cradled in its arms. She cocked her head first one way and then the other and wrinkled her nose as if she smelled something bad.

"Yeah, well," he said. What was he supposed to say? Was he supposed to defend himself or what? "If you put it that way, yes, it is silly, but then look at your T-shirt."

"My T-shirt?" she laughed. "My T-shirt? What's that got to do with anything?"

"Well, isn't that silly?"

"Yes, but it's meant to be."

"And your hair."

"My hair?" she squawked, giving the last word two syllables.

"Yeah. Why did you get it all curled like that? Isn't that silly?"

She touched a handful of curls thoughtfully and frowned.

"Oh, I see," she said finally.

"You see what?"

"Anything else?"

"What?"

"Anything else you want to criticize about me? My shoes? The size of my hips? This skirt? My face? Meet with your approval, do they?"

"No, that's not what I meant."

"Oh, sure."

"No, listen."

"Don't bother. I ask a simple little question and you just launch into a personal attack."

"No. It wasn't that. I meant that everything's silly when you come to think..."

"What? What?"

"You know, if you take an existentialist view point."

She frowned at him, "Oh, that's right. Mystify everything with big words. Why don't you just sod off," she said and gave Eve an almighty rattle which caused the serpent to leap into the air in a curiously life-like way and crash to the floor.

Paul was so impressed with the aerodynamics of its flight; the convincing way it had twisted and rippled, that he just stood for some time with his mouth agape.

"There," Karen said defiantly. "Now look what you've made me do." She gently pushed at the snake with her toe. "Poor little worm," she whispered, then watched the head loll gracelessly as the V-shaped tongue clattered tinnily like a broken bell.

Poor little worm. Hah, Paul thought, the truth's coming out now.

He watched her. She knelt and scooped up the little broken body with its head hanging down.

"Can you fix it?" she asked quietly and looked up at him with an expression of exaggerated humility. Her eyes were big, and glittered as if tears were about to well over.

He knelt down beside her and lifted the serpent's head in the palm of his hand as if he were weighing it.

"I guess I can bring him back to life," he said quietly. Then leaning awkwardly forward he tilted his lips towards hers and they kissed with the snake still held delicately between them like a baby.

And everything had seemed okay then. He'd said "I love your hair. I love your face. I love you from the top of your head to the tips of your toes," and she frowned with a pretend expression of crossness on her face and said "Really?" and he'd said, "Yes. Really I do," and kissed her again to prove it.

That had been three weeks ago, and while he'd continued to melt into her and to feel happier in her presence than when alone, her words kept coming back. "Isn't it just silly? Isn't it silly? Silly, silly, daft and silly?"

He finished Eve by adding long coils of copper wire as hair and started work on Adam. He had decided that he would create Adam in his own image. He had wanted to tell Karen about this, but each time the thought occurred he suppressed it. He'd collect her from her house and they'd stroll with their arms around each other down the hill to the pub. The evenings were warm and she'd feel soft and fragile under his touch. She'd chat about her job, tell him gossip about her flatmates, make plans for holidays they'd take, or records she wanted to buy, and in reply he'd "Mmm" or smile.

He meanwhile was living in a little dictator state where there was heavy censorship. No talk about art, was the state's slogan. Phrases would pop into his consciousness ready to be spoken aloud. Phrases like "Well, today I made Adam a breastplate from a car fender" or "I was going to do loads of work today, but the damn welder packed up on me." He could almost sense these words marching to the end of his brain like eager little citizens ready to leap onto his tongue and escape out into the world.

"Halt," the official censor would say, "Halt. No trespass. Go back to your home, little words or it'll be the water cannon for you."

"So," Karen would say, snuggling closer after he'd brought the drinks over from the bar, "how was your day?"

"Well," he'd say, taking a sip of beer and searching for a suitable answer, "okay. Okay... how about you?" and she'd launch into some complicated story about her boss. Then later there'd be some lull in the conversation and he'd find himself sifting through his mental scrap heap searching for an eye-shaped cog, and he'd want to say "Karen, do you think a cog with a marble attached would make a good eye?" but instead he'd say again, to fill the gaping silence, "So, how was your day?"

"Paul. You've already asked me that."

"Oh. Did I?"

"Yes. God, you're going senile. You really are."

But then she'd remember something and she'd be off again, "Oh, but have I told you about what Simone did yesterday?"

And he'd hear all about Simone and their landlady and the rent increase and every passing rain cloud that had set out just to rain on Karen's parade.

He bit his tongue. Not literally of course, but metaphorically.

He thought about the expression. Did anyone actually bite their tongue? People did, by accident, of course. He could remember numerous occasions when he'd done it as a child – usually when he'd been eating something with a bit too much enthusiasm and too little care. Or once when he'd been whacked on the chin by a cricket bat. That had hurt, had even drawn blood and he'd licked his lips giving them a smear of vampirish gore which had made his clumsy batting friend go pale, and had made the girls scream. At other times he'd bitten the fleshy inside of his lips which had produced a sort of meaty swelling which he'd chewed on, so that instead of going away, it had got worse and worse until his mother had to take him to the doctor.

He remembered his first aid training; how when confronted by the thrashing victim of epilepsy, you had to do something important to their tongue, but what was it? Somehow, he seemed to think, what you had to do was hold their tongue because they'd just go and swallow it and then choke to death. Could you swallow your tongue? He tried it, but it seemed impossible. And could you, for that matter, hold onto a tongue? Wasn't it just too slippery to get a grip on it? Forgetting himself for a moment and frowning with concentration, he attempted this. His tongue slipped from his fingers. He tried again, this time with two hands.

"Paul, people are staring. What the hell are you doing?"

"Urumph," he pulled his fingers from his mouth, "oh, nothing, nothing."

Karen frowned at him. His fingers were gooky with spit. He wiped them on his jeans. Karen continued to stare.

"What?"

"Paul, you are dribbling."

Sure enough, one stubborn little string of saliva was hanging from his lower lip. He wiped it away with the back of his hand.

"Okay?" he asked, presenting his face for her approval.

"Were you always this weird? Did you hide it from me or have I only just noticed?"

"I hid it," he said, reaching for her hand and laughing, but she pulled her hand away.

"Yuk. Don't touch me – you've slobbered all over that hand."

"So?"

"It's disgusting."

"You don't say that when I kiss you."

"Yeah, well."

"What?"

"How could I say anything when you've got your bloody tongue in my mouth?"

"Hey, hang on, what are you saying? That you don't like the way I kiss you?"

"Just forget it."

"Just forget it? Forget it? How can I forget it?"

"Try. I'm going to the loo."

With that Karen got up and headed for the toilets. She was wearing a black T-shirt with a white and red target printed on it. He stared after her. Looking daggers, he thought. Stab in the back. Bite your tongue.

She seemed in a better mood when she came back. She'd applied a fresh coat of red lipstick and gave him a dazzling smile.

He melted.

Later he walked her home and when she opened the front door he made to follow her in as usual.

"Not tonight," she said barring his way.

"Oh."

"Let's just cool it a bit, for a while."

"But..."

"Really. I'll ring you later in the week."

"If that's what you want."

She turned to go, but he grabbed her hand and pulled her gently to him, "Hey, we haven't said 'goodnight'."

She sighed, but submitted to his embrace. He hugged her and gave her a little peck on the lips.

"Goodnight Karen."

"Night," she said quickly, but he still held her.

"Oh Karen," he murmured and squeezed her tighter as he planted his lips over hers. Blissfully he closed his eyes. His tongue, remembering its naughty habits took a joyful leap in to the warm velvet void of her open mouth. He thought "Oh, Karen, such a girl. I could kiss you forever." That was when she decided enough was enough, and brought her teeth together, and captured his tongue and held it.

"Neugh," he said, "neugh."

He opened his eyes and saw, in close up, the blurry multiples that were Karen's eyes; like a spider's. She wasn't biting hard enough to cause him pain, but just enough to hold him there.

"Kawun," he managed to say. "Kawun, pleath."

She let go and he reached for his mouth defensively. He licked his palms and checked them for blood.

Karen stood leaning against the door jamb, arms folded and smirking.

"What d'you do that for?"

"What did I do what for?" she said with a triumphant expression on her face.

"Bite me," he said indignantly.

"You want me to bite you?"

"No. What did you bite me for?"

"That wasn't a bite – that's just the way I kiss. Like it? Anyway, must go, night-night." And she shut the door.

Paul ran his fingers over his tongue searching for indentation, scarring or other permanent injury. He studied his fingers for minute particles of blood.

Nothing. And neither was there that familiar and chillingly metallic taste of blood to be detected anywhere.

Crouching, he pushed open the letterbox and peered into the hall. The light was still on and he thought he could hear someone laughing. As he watched the light went out. Delicately he eased the letterbox shut.

He sighed with resignation and made for home. "Oh, Karen," he thought, and felt a sense of loss sharply. But, by the time he had reached the end of her road and turned onto the high street, he was distracted by other thoughts. These were: new ways with welding, plots about exhibitions, a new sculpture – Pandora and her box of evil. Or Icarus with hinged, movable wings. Or.

"Ah, if there were scrap enough or time…" he mused, deliberately misquoting Andrew Marvell. "Silly indeed," he remembered ruefully, "I'll show her who's silly" and he embarked on a glorious fantasy of his spectacular first exhibition and Karen having to push her way through the adoring crowds to get near to him.

"It's me," she'd say, "me. Karen. Remember?"

He'd "hmm" thoughtfully and she'd look at him pleadingly, then in a loud, clear voice she'd say, "Paul, I was wrong. You *are* a genius. I was a foolish girl – forgive me."

Naturally, he'd be gentle with her; lift her from her knees and say something consoling. Someone close by would say "Truly he is a great man." Oddly this always came out sounding like John Wayne in that old technicolour biblical film. "Oh well," he thought, then he ran and re-ran the fantasy reel until it grew scratched and faded and artificial.

He began to think about a news article he'd recently read about old celluloid film stock deteriorating in store rooms; becoming brittle and turning to dust. He remembered other things he'd read, like what happened when the tombs of the Pharoahs were opened up to the rush of hot new desert air. He imagined being Howard Carter, or whoever, in a pith helmet and sand-coloured safari suit, reaching for some beautiful artifact, and seeing it crumble in his fingers.

It seemed impossible that so much human labour; so many dreams and hopes could so easily turn to dust. What if, he wondered, one tiny atom from the tombs had swirled into the air and travelled by some weird miracle across continents and oceans into the still night around him?

He lapped the air with his tongue and tasted the bitter sulphur of mortality.

Or maybe, he thought, growing suddenly light hearted, maybe it's just stale beer and no mystery whatsoever.

Seven Thousand Flowers

In Mannheim, Germany, the Youth Hostel is full of travellers. It is August, and August reminds the Youth Hostel keeper of sin in a way that the other months of the year cannot. He is an old man now, so for him, sin is far beyond its first blush.

He lives every summer surrounded by the youths of many nations. The dark-haired Italian girls, the blonde Swedes and big boned Danes, the jabbering small-breasted Japanese, the earthy British girls and dull Germans. He finds the Germans dull because their excited small talk and big boasts come to his ears as a language instead of noise. He is assailed and disappointed by their words, "I'm going to wear my pink socks, what do you think?" "Oh, look there's Wolfgang. Ah, he's looking at Gabi." "Do I look fat in this?" "Lend me your shampoo, Eva."

It is Gunter's job to assign duties to the various school parties who visit. He always sends the Germans upstairs to sweep dormitories and swab bathrooms, and in that way he keeps the foreigners close by in the kitchen and the downstairs.

Gunter's wife has been dead now for eleven years and while he publicly mourns her, secretly he is glad that she is dead and buried. Every week he takes flowers and places them on her grave. For this he is respected by the minister and the congregation of his parish. They expect that when death comes to him he will be laid in the same grave as her. They think that he is a man who loved deeply and long, a believer in heaven and its promise of reunion in death. Ha, if only they knew the joy he feels, as he pulls the dripping half-rotted stems of last week's flowers from the stone pot and replaces them with fresh ones.

Gunter is particularly fond of foxgloves. In the grounds of the Youth Hostel he grows these at the back of the flowerbeds, with smaller flowers: marigolds, lobelia, busy lizzies, salvia and violets, in front. He grows vegetables too. Runner beans that twist their way up bamboo poles. Tomatoes in the greenhouse and fat marrow that lie plumply on the ground and remind him of Marta in her favourite green-striped summer frock. Add a head and fat stumpy arms and legs, and yes, that is Marta, who was too clever for her own good.

If he'd known of her talent for languages he'd never have married her. But Marta, the fleshless displaced person ten years older than him whom he found wandering the streets of Graz, spoke alien words which came to his ears like sweet music. Then, very quickly, she grew fat on the German tongue. By 1950 she spoke like a native, but by then it was too late for Gunter to escape. She gave him six sons and all of them took after her with thick mahogany hair and strong compact physiques. Gunter was fair and wiry, and imagined his sons had grown inside his wife's body like curious mushrooms erupting from spores in the dank and dark of her womb.

He had no affection for the boys, though he played at the pretence of love well, boasting in the beer garden and reciting their names and pulling their pictures from his wallet for all who cared to see.

They lived modestly, as Gunter was never able to find a very well paid job due to his inability to take orders or get along with his work-mates. But the fruits and vegetables he grew kept them well fed, and even when they lived in the flat that overlooked the steelworks, Gunter would manage to grow a few tomatoes and strawberries, and herbs in the window boxes. Marta went often to visit her sister who lived near the forest in the west and would bring home eggs and smoked meats, and wild blackberries and mushrooms of every sort and dimension.

How he hated mushrooms. He hated them as much as they,

his wife and sons, loved them. As soon as he saw Marta unwrapping a giant puff-ball from a tea towel and getting the knife in readiness to slice it like some huge haunch of meat, he would be gone. He could not bear the smell of it frying in the pan, the butter blackened and the garlic burnt. Marta, it seemed, was determined to poison him. She'd sneak mushrooms into almost every dish she cooked, she mashed them and puréed them and urged him to, please, just taste this one or give that one a chance. She would describe their different flavours; this one is like nuts, this like aniseed, but Gunter could not be tempted.

Their six sons broke Marta's heart when each one left home and settled down in countries far away from Germany. Two were in America, one in Canada, one in England, one in Denmark and one in Finland. All, except one wrote letters home to Marta with long declarations of love, everyday news and most importantly, details of the mushrooms they had hunted down and eaten which, they said, reminded them of home more than all the photos and words could ever do.

Marta had not been well for many years. At the beginning of the war she had contracted tuberculosis. Then when she was pregnant with their last son she had developed diabetes. Later came arthritis and two bouts of pneumonia. She no longer travelled on the train to her sister's house. No longer wandered the woods and the pastures with her sharp knife and her basket, plucking honeycombed morels and whale-gilled oyster mushrooms and mustard coloured Chanterelles.

The margins of her life narrowed and shrank, until at last, she was unable to leave the house and finally unable to leave her bedroom, except to make the slow and agonizing journey to the bathroom with her zimmer frame leading the way.

But, good news, good news, the doctor said, with care she could live for another ten or twenty years. Gunter smiled and took the latest pictures of his sons and grandchildren from his wallet. He bragged about their impressive professions, this one a Doctor of Botany, this one an airline pilot, this one a graphic designer and so on. The doctor laid a hand on Gunter's shoulder and told him he was blessed. And Gunter bemoaned his poor housekeeping skills; cobwebs in the high corners of the ceiling, porcelain figurines whose features were unrecognizable under layers of dust, meals of tinned soup and plain boiled potatoes which poor Marta barely touched. Try to tempt her, said the doctor, learn to cook her favourites, do this with love and she'll thrive.

Downstairs, Gunter and the doctor drank imported whisky from smeared glasses. The doctor was used to the houses of the sick, the musty smells of disordered bodies and souls, he knew that both the sick and those who cared for them deserved this extra five minutes of his time. He listened then, as Gunter told him of his wife's old love of mushrooms and asked whether fungi was health giving. The doctor repeated his words about tempting her to eat, about the Christian symbolism of food, the relationship between food and love. Fine words, he later thought, fine words indeed.

At the inquest into Marta's death, the doctor bowed his head with shame as he repeated those enthusiastic words, and told how he had urged Gunter to cook her the mushrooms. Tears poured down Gunter's creased face; rivers that ran through gullies, coursed around moles, trickled through the forest on his upper lip and chin. He wrung his hands, cursed himself, cursed God, cursed the forest and the deception of its fruits.

He was told by everyone that he should not, must not, blame himself. They said that perhaps it was a mercy, that Marta was now released from this vale of tears: her suffering was over, and he, Gunter, must be strong for the sake of his sons.

So Gunter grew flowers, and went to her graveside and cut away the weeds, and cleaned the stone memorial which his son the architect had paid for. And he made sure that his pilgrimage to the graveside was seen by as many people as possible.

Eleven years was a lot of flowers. Maybe as many as seven thousand stems. An army of flowers that protected Gunter. Flowers which held him upright in the eyes of his neighbours, made him a sad victim of circumstance; for was he not the man who had killed his wife with love?

And now he has this job at the Youth Hostel, with its fine grounds in which he can grow seven thousand more flowers, and listen to the babbling of foreign tongues drifting in the twilight from the open windows of the dormitories. And he can stand in the garden, with the hoe or rake in his old man's twisted hands, dirt beneath the nails, and see the flitting figures of the girls running about in bras and petticoats. Or he can stand in the corridor with his steaming mop while they run laughing from the bathroom with only a towel wrapped around their glistening torsos. Damp flesh like petals dotted with dew.

Gunter makes the pretence of mourning as skillfully as he once made the pretence of love. Everyone believes in it, except for his six clever sons. But any doubts, connected as they are to memories of their cold, uncaring and distant father remain as mere spores, buried beneath the colourful gardens of their successful lives. They find that now they each have wives and children of their own, that there is little to bring them back to Germany and the dutiful visits are postponed again and again.

It's a bad show, this tendency of his sons to never visit him. He writes them pitiful letters, begging them to come, but he cannot let go of that tone he always uses, forgets to mention how much he'd like to see them, forgets the names of their wives and children, and says instead how alone he is, how the neighbours are talking.

One day, after hours in the garden planting tender young seedlings with the sun beating down on his bald spot, he staggers into the sudden dark of the entrance hall of the hostel, and standing there, waiting for their teachers, is a party of school girls. Gunter does not see girls of thirteen or fourteen. What Gunter sees is a row of tall flowers, the most beautiful flowers he has ever seen. Flowers with soft petal heads that bob in a gentle breeze and speak to him in a special flower language. He reaches out to touch. The flowers shriek with alarm and run from him and his mud-smeared hands.

Confused, Gunter stumbles back into the garden. The sun is setting and the sky is bleeding blue, red, lilac, orange, crimson, mauve. He feels dizzy, the world is swooping around him, spinning on its axis, toying with him. Gunter falls amongst the flower beds, the band across his chest tightening like the encroaching bindweed that is choking and crushing him as surely as it does his flowers.

The foxgloves bend their heavy dusky heads towards him and he thinks he hears them whisper rhythmically: digitalis, digitalis, digitalis. But the flowers' concern has come too late for the gardener, and the earth below seems to sigh in readiness for its feast.

Peaches

I don't know why my mother told me our true family history at the particular time she chose. There seemed no reason for it. I'd suspected nothing and hadn't been asking questions. I suppose she'd been turning it around in her head for all those years, letting it grow ripe until it was full and plump and soft and close to the point of bursting.

The day she told me was hot – a real scorcher, and I was out in the back garden lying on a scratchy old tartan blanket. I had the top-twenty on the radio, so it must have been a Sunday. I'd shouted for her to come out and bring me a drink, and to put some more sun oil on my back. She came, carrying a tray laden with the lemonade I'd asked for, a gin and tonic for herself and a plate of sandwiches made just how I liked them: cut into triangles with the crusts off and a little sprig of parsley crowning them. There were also some nice fresh peaches, which I reached for first. I picked the fattest, juiciest-looking one and turned it over in my hand, occasionally bringing it to my nose so that I could breathe in the sweet promise of its flesh while enjoying the tactile sensation of its furred skin. I glanced at my mother. She was watching me and grimacing. For her the surface of a peach was like the scratch of a fingernail on a blackboard. Her look, I must admit, made me caress the peach all the more.

"Ai! How can you do that!" she shuddered. In reply I bit in.

I was wearing my first bikini which was made of black shiny nylon. The garden must have been the one which belonged to the house in Ealing. The one that overlooked the common. Because I remember that after my mother unburdened her dreadful secrets, I sat unmovingly in the twilight listening to the distant and joyous screams and the rattle of machinery and the hum of generators and the thumping distorted bass of the music from the fair. So it must have been August of 1978; the summer when I turned 15 and had my first boyfriend, first bra and first cigarette.

I was at that age when I'd begun to call my mother by her Christian name – a thing she resented by the looks she flashed me when I said it, but as she never actually forbade it I carried on in my own sweet way. I was, I suppose, at that most difficult of ages, desperate to shed myself of childhood, to shake myself free, but yet filled with the arrogance and ennui of barely tarnished innocence.

Maybe mother could sense my transformation approaching, could smell it in the air or see it glittering darkly in my eyes. Perhaps that was why she acted when she did, catching me on the brink of change and holding me there with her secrets.

So, there I was in the garden, fifteen years old. Small breasted and skinny in a bikini built for a woman. Thinking I knew it all and about to discover that I actually knew nothing. About to learn that truth was a variable; a mere surface, like the flawless skin of a ripe fruit which hides a maggot.

"Eleanor," said my mother, "there's something I have to tell you."

I sighed distractedly and undid my bikini top so that she could rub the oil in my back. I folded my arms in front of my chest in order to keep my breasts securely hidden, though there was no one to see them besides her.

"It's something you have to know. It will make you understand. It's about me and your grandmother really."

All I had said to this was "Is this going to take a long time? Because I was going to go around Patrick's later to do some work on our project."

"Oh, that boy," said my mother with agony in her voice and I thought she was going to give me her usual lecture about

Patrick and "nice boys" and my reputation and getting into trouble, but instead she'd said, "I'll be as brief as I can." So I resigned myself to listening, at least for a short while.

She began, "My father was...." then stopped herself. "Oh! How to tell it? Your grandfather, he was.... No, no, no. Now listen, you know that I was born in France in 1944? About the time of the liberation?"

"Yes," I said, putting all the boredom and sarcasm I could muster into my voice, but she chose to ignore this and carried on. Unstoppable, like she'd sometimes be.

"The war years were very hard – it wasn't like it seems in the history books. It wasn't just soldiers and leaders. It was surviving day after day, getting by any way you could. There's nothing neat about it. War is a mess. It was not knowing what's going to happen. Imagine growing up in all that, being a young girl, wanting all those things that young girls want, wanting love."

"So?" I said archly. "You didn't live through that, you were just a baby."

In reply my mother merely gave a long drawn out sigh, took her hands from my back and tapped my shoulder twice to signal she'd done with the sun oil.

"I'm telling you how it was, just like my mother told me."

I reached around to do up my bikini again, sliding my fingers over the hot slippery surface of my back, then I turned to face her. She was rhythmically wiping the fingers of one hand on the edge of the rug and her head was bent down with her left hand clasped over her mouth, as if she wanted to silence herself. I thought I'd better shut up and listen or I'd never get to Patrick's and it was important I get to Patrick's that day as his family were away for the weekend.

So I said, to placate her, "Please, tell me, Mum. Please."

My mother lifted her head and I saw that her eyes were swimming in tears. Maybe it was me calling her "Mum" again that softened her, went straight to her heart like a knife. Maybe that's how it was with mothers, you only had to say "Mum" or "please" and they melted into the old clinging memories of hope.

"I wish," she began then, "I wish I didn't have to tell you, but you must know."

I nodded sympathetically.

"Your grandfather was a soldier...."

Well, this I knew. Wasn't that why we'd ended up in England? Hadn't there been the liberation and D-day and the soldiers, both American and British, swarming over France? All of them lonely khaki heroes finding grateful love in the arms of pretty French women? Wasn't that what liberation was all about? Bottles of champagne and Pernod and dark red Claret uncovered from secret cellars to bless the lips and tongues of these laughing and hungry men? And everyone drunk on freedom and the sky an endless blue; laughter easy and language among the Babel of races reduced to signs and kisses and beckoning fingers; the gestures of pleasure in food and wine and love.

I had always thought that it was quite romantic the way my grandmother and grandfather had met, the way he'd brought her back to England like a trophy of war. Despite the big difference in their ages, the gulf between her youth and beauty and his lack of any discernable charms. Although I must admit that into certain dark shadows of untold detail I'd always painted my own bright colours. There was also the problem of dates, of birth and marriage. I suspected that my mother might be illegitimate, but what did it matter? It made everything all the more interesting. "Now," I had thought, "now she's going to admit it."

"Your grandfather's name was Holger Herzog."

I stared dumbly at my mother. At first only taking in the information that this was not the name of the man I always called "Grandpa". This was not the blunt Yorkshireman called Archibald Bratley who masqueraded in the role of grandfather to this day; sitting in his armchair by the fire, chafing his hands together and saying, "Make another brew, pet. I'm parched."

I imagined this was exactly what he was doing at that very moment. While my grandmother, accent still so thick you could cut it with a good French kitchen knife, would be scuttling off to the kitchen and obediently rattling the kettle, teapot and cups into service.

But then, the name. The name! Holger Herzog! This was no French name. This name was surely German.

The sun disappeared behind a small single cloud and no sooner had our eyes adjusted to the shadowless world than it appeared again, blinding and dazzling us. I blinked at mother and shaded my eyes. My breath came in shallow gasps. "Oh God," I had said, "oh god."

Mother watched me. She looked ashamed, like a child caught out in a lie. "I am so sorry," she whispered.

I wanted to get away from her. I wanted at that instant to be transported to Patrick's house. I wanted to be in his arms in the big hammock on the patio that overlooked his parents' garden; to tell him this thing, this terrible thing and cry and be comforted. Even then I imagined it more as my mother's delusion than anything like truth.

Instead, I listened to my mother's words – what else could I do? And let her distractedly stroke the soles of my feet and ankles like she used to when I was little.

Later she called for a taxi for me to go to Patrick's and stood on the pavement under the trees waving sadly as the cab drew away. I sat there watching as she shrank into the distance and the shadows, and I rehearsed my first words to Patrick. I imagined myself falling into his arms, sobbing and faint as his concern and love washed over me.

I imagined many things during that short journey as I held myself hunched up in the corner of the cab, my head pressed hard against the dirty cool glass of its window. Most of them to do with Patrick.

Patrick's family seemed to me to be very rich, though Patrick, echoing his parents, said they were merely "comfortable". They lived in a large 1930's mock-Tudor mansion in a quiet leafy avenue near Walpole Park. His father did something for the BBC and his mother played the cello and both were, consequently, often away on business or tours. Their house was like something out of *Ideal Home* magazine. I couldn't imagine how anyone could live in such spotless perfection. It was as if their lives glided over the surface of everything without substance, as if their glands sent forth polish instead of sweat.

Patrick, their only child, was the sole blemish under their roof. His hair was cropped on top so that it stood up on end and reminded me of a hedgehog's back, except that when you touched it, it was soft. He wore old men's home-knitted sweaters that were always about three or four sizes too big and whose sleeves and necks ended in ragged loose ends of trailing wool. He spoke with a lazy cockney accent and his voice was husky from too many cigarettes.

When he came to the door he was wearing dark glasses with mirror lenses so that when I looked for his eyes all I saw was my face, pig-like, reflected back at me. Somehow in the taxi I'd imagined that my tears and the telling of my misery would just happen, but once there in the cool hall with him, I felt numb and dry; shrivelled somehow.

As soon as Patrick had shut the front door he put his arms around me and I, in return, wrapped my arms around his waist and put my head against his chest and shut my eyes. I could feel the plastic of his sunglasses digging into my head as he rested his head on mine. We stood like that for a long time swaying from side to side; almost, but not quite, dancing. It dawned on me as I stood there that this thing I wanted to tell him, this miserable truth that weighed on me was all wrong. I wanted his comfort and pity but I was on the wrong side. I wasn't on the side of the victims, or even the heroes, I was now the aggressor. Either that or I was the daughter of a mad woman.

I kept remembering the figure of my mother under the trees outside our house – her small head and tiny body and raven black hair which she wore in tight, Shirley Temple curls which gave her the appearance of a shrunken doll. She embarrassed me. She'd embarrassed me for as long as I could remember but until now I didn't know why. I thought it was those insignificant things like her stupid hairstyle, her continual fussing over me, the way she could never keep a man, the frown marks between her eyes, her slow and hesitant way of speaking.

I considered this as I stood rocking gently, but this other image of my mother kept clouding my resentment. Well, not an image so much as a smell and that smell was eau de Cologne on warm skin. But it wasn't just a smell either, it was also a feeling; a feeling of security. And a place I'd been once. I felt tired suddenly; mesmerized by the black and white checkerboard of tiles swaying at my feet. Against my hip I could feel some hard part of Patrick pressed and his breath was hot on my neck. With some awkwardness I lifted my face towards his and pecked at his cheek leaving the imprint of my lipstick there. He responded by finding my mouth and holding me tighter.

I always shut my eyes when we kissed and I assumed that he had also removed himself to some blind place where sensation depended on touch and taste and sound and smell alone. Patrick and I were quite expert at kissing; that liquid drilling of our mouths and the tight press of our bodies. We could do it for hour after hour and frequently did. Standing up or sitting side by side with our bodies twisted at the waist towards each other or lying stretched full length. I had been waiting for the next stage which, I assumed, would be set in motion by Patrick, as he was the male and the elder and more experienced. This next stage would be the opening of my blouse, the unclasping of my bra, the coldness of his hand on the hot swell of my breast. Whenever I thought about this I would shiver deliciously and butterflies would leap and claw at the pit of my belly. But after six months all I had known of Patrick was the swirling tongue and the mysterious press of his body. I was beginning to doubt him, to not trust the looks and kisses. Yet when he put his arm around my neck it felt right, cool like water, part of me but not part of me.

I entertained myself as we stood there endlessly kissing, by wondering whether kissing felt the same for everyone? Whether another boy would be completely different? How it felt for Patrick to kiss me? And, disturbingly, whether it had felt like this when my grandmother had kissed her German soldier? It was just as that last question rose in my mind that Patrick gathered all the courage and passion he'd been storing up for six months and without warning clamped his hand clumsily on my right breast.

My reaction was electric. It was as if the German, my supposed grandfather (bearer, upholder and celebrant of the ugliest episode in recent history possible) had lifted his claw in France and brought it down upon my breast over thirty years later. I leapt back gasping and opened my eyes to see poor Patrick – a look of absolute horror on his face. My own face, I reasoned, must have worn a mirror image of his expression. Or worse, exposed this terrible heritage of mine, the inherited cruelty and destruction, the love of marching and killing, the blue of my eyes, the grey of my heart.

I turned and made for the stairs, walking at first, then running, taking the steps two or three at a time. Finally I plunged into the bathroom, slamming and bolting the door behind me. It was quiet up there. Quiet and cool as all sanctuaries should be. The bathroom, like the rest of the house, was immaculate, everything seemed to have been carefully arranged. From the colour co-ordinated towels on the rail to the orderly ranks of expensive bath oil and perfume, to the trailing stems and leaves of palms and ivy and spider plants which seemed to curl or fall or stab the air in artful shapes which belied nature.

I lay down on the carpet studying the ceiling while tears ran down the sides of my face and gathered in pools around my ears, trying to stifle my louder sobs. I knew that sooner or later Patrick would come to find me.

Eventually, the door handle was gently turned. I heard a soft, hesitant tapping at the door, then Patrick's voice, "Ellie? Are you OK? I'm sorry. El? Can you hear me? I'm sorry."

Back in the garden at home my mother had told me that

the man who had fathered her wasn't all bad. That not all Germans had been bad. Not even all the German soldiers. She said that maybe, somehow the fact that love could still happen even in circumstances like that meant that life was worthwhile. I was disgusted by her using the word "love" like that. I thought she used it just to soften the truth. Or even, God forbid, to romanticize this thing.

Then she told me, and by then I was trying not to listen, trying not to hear or care or remember any of it, what had happened to Holger Herzog.

Though first she said, "Do you know how old this soldier was? He was just seventeen years old. The same age as that Patrick boy." I was surprised by that, but somehow I couldn't quite erase the dreadful image I'd created of a brutish man snarling his thick-necked guttural language into the vulnerable world and trailing destruction in his black-booted wake.

The villagers had caught him and my grandma hiding in a barn, "clinging to each other like Hansel and Gretel", my mother said. They'd been wrenched apart and he had been dragged through the peach orchard by the leaders of the resistance and, helped by a small group of drunken Allied soldiers, he'd been strung from the highest tree.

As she spoke, I could not help imagining (and perhaps this was a form of self-protection, a process by which everything became a fiction as unreal as a comic strip) the rope around Patrick's throat, his neck fine and soft and delicate as a girl's, twisted and pinched by the noose. And his eyes wet with tears, fearful, tortured, knowing the end of his life was only minutes away. And beneath their feet, the wind-fallen fruits were crushed, their broken flesh giving off sickly sweet perfume.

Then she had told me what had been done to my grandmother; the clumsy shaving of her head, the threats, the way they had marched her around the town and spat at her. But worst of all they'd made her watch him die. She felt she had killed him.

My mother and I had sat quietly after all those words, both

of us exhausted. Then she'd said, "How many wrongs, do you think, it takes to make a right?"

I stood up and turned on the cold tap and splashed my face with water. I picked up one of the bottles of scent from the glass shelf and unscrewed the cap and tipped the bottle against one wrist, then rubbed my wrist against my neck. I felt better then, ready to face Patrick again.

I unlocked the bathroom door and there he was. The dark glasses were gone and his eyes looked red, as if he had been crying. He said, "I'm really sorry, El." I put my arms around him and said, "It wasn't that," and to prove it I took his hand and guided it under my T-shirt and placed it on my breast and he let out a little sigh that could have been pleasure and could have been relief.

"Come on," said Patrick, taking hold of my hand, before leading me out of the bathroom and down the stairs, "let's listen to some music." We walked together towards the back of the house to a room I hadn't been in before. At the door Patrick stopped and said, "The best stereo is in here, this is the old girl's music room," before kneeling down at my feet and unfastening my sandals, "so you have to take your shoes off." He smiled up at me as I stood there barefoot, my eyes still stinging from all the crying I'd done, as he gently ran his fingers over my calves and an inch or so up my thighs. Then he stood and opened the door and ushered me in with a sweeping gesture.

I entered a room that was almost entirely white. The carpet was white, the walls were white, the fireplace a high snowy marble one whose streaks of silver and black merely emphasized the whiteness of the rest. The end of the room was dominated by a huge window hung with curtains of white muslin, in front of which was a white grand piano.

The only things which had any colour were the records – shelf after shelf – and the sheet music and the framed concert posters and photographs. A cello was propped by the grand like a squat, brown-skinned soprano waiting for the appearance of the pianist. It balanced its bulk on one impossibly slim leg.

I would have liked to touch it, to have drawn some noise from it no doubt, some violence on the untarnished air. Or better, I would have liked to have sat straddling its hourglass figure and to take up the bow and find, by some curious magic, that music, low and throbbing, swept from my sawing fingers. But I dared not. Instead, while Patrick ran upstairs to get some albums from his bedroom, I strolled around the room, studying everything. There were piles of sheet music, some of it clearly very old. I opened one at random and ran my eye along rows of an alien language; the crotchets and quavers and semi-quavers whose connection and translation into the sounds of horn or violin or cello seemed, to me, an impossible miracle. I felt like an intruder in this room – everything about it was too pure and I half understood the destruction wreaked by burglars in rooms like this. Yet I also felt a part of it all as if my relationship with Patrick gave me licence, made me valid, made me more than myself.

One wall of the room was almost entirely filled from floor to ceiling with posters, photographs, programmes, and news cuttings. Each had its own frame and while these were of different shapes, styles and colours, the cacophony of their patchwork arrangement made a whole. I began to look more carefully, reading names, dates, details.

At one end, nearest the window, I found a face of the woman I knew as Patrick's mother. Her hair was the colour that played it safe, occupying the territory which existed between a young sensual platinum blond and a more staid and sensible white. It was long and she wore it drawn back, either, as on the day that I met her, in a silvery ponytail, or for more formal occasions, in an upswept bun or chignon. In the most recent photograph she was accepting an award of some sort and smiling a Mona Lisa smile at a man in evening dress as he handed her some shiny metal thing on a small plinth. Above that was a brightly coloured poster which advertised "Summer in the City: a series of lunchtime recitals in the Barbican Centre". Patrick's mother was listed to play on Saturday the 5th of May of that year.

As I progressed down the wall the clippings from newspapers became more yellowed and the style of the posters more staid, and his mother's face shed the years; growing smoother skin and more clearly defined bones, shaking her hair loose and letting its golden highlights shine more brightly. Halfway down the wall she even shed her name. Now, no longer did she call herself Rachel Murphy. Instead she went by the name of Rachel Greenberg and there she was, a tiny slip of a girl posing with a nervous smile (gone was the knowing Mona Lisa), her hair in two long plaits, on the gangplank of a ship with the unmistakable bulk of a cello case beside her. Beneath, the caption read, "Child protégé flees Nazi Europe."

That afternoon in the garden with my mother seemed a long time ago. I sensed that from that moment on, my life would always be divided between knowing and not knowing, innocence (intoxicating, blind sweet innocence) and knowledge. I remembered that last glimpse of my mother under the trees and her secret seemed like a black hole which sucked everything in upon itself. I remembered too, her hand raised; the palm offered, in not so much a wave of farewell, as a gesture that meant stop.

Patrick, on finding Eleanor standing quietly looking at the picture collection, crept up behind her and gently put one arm around her waist. He felt her stomach contract beneath his fingers and her hands moved to rest on his. With his free hand he drew the hair from her neck. She smelt sweet and her skin was warm; the nape of her neck softly furred with fine pale hair. He put his mouth there and licked, but his tongue found a bitter chemical taint and he was disappointed. He'd imagined she'd taste like she smelled – of peaches.

Home-cooked

My daughter has been living with her father for the past three months. She used to live with me and he lived close by, so that every weekend and some weeknights too, she'd see him. But then he had to go and move away. Had to take a job on the other side of the country, like he couldn't have stayed put, couldn't have managed somehow, for our sake, for her sake.

Now she's back for the summer, and I feel suddenly like I'm entertaining a stranger, that she's just some stray teenager who's come into my life. A lodger who doesn't pay rent, who spends hours on the phone, demands food at odd hours, sneers at me, and then to top it all demands money. She's like the Mafia, except that the tribute I pay is for her protection, not mine.

In the time she's been gone, while she was changing, growing taller and acquiring a certain chill maturity, I've been remembering who I was when I was younger. I've been going out more, doing those impossibly spontaneous things like going for drinks after work with colleagues. That's how I got together with Simon, who I'd worked with for years, but had barely spoken a word to.

Tonight was Simon's idea. A way for my daughter and him to get to know each other. He doesn't know it but I had to bribe her to come with us. That outfit she's wearing is brand new. She said she couldn't come because she had nothing to wear. Needed something smart if we were going to a fancy restaurant. And she'd smiled a sweet hopeful smile and in that smile I'd seen this perfect family outing, her with hair freshly washed, and just a little make-up, and a pretty dress, perhaps. What she's wearing though is a pair of the biggest flares I've ever seen, and a black belt with evil-looking silver studs, and a T-shirt that says "Porn Star" in big letters across the chest.

We take a taxi into town, and go to Wind Street, and begin to search for somewhere nice to eat. It's Sunday night and I imagine it'll be easy to find somewhere, but a lot of the places won't let under eighteens in. We're doing a lot of walking

There used to be just three or four pubs on this street. Four pubs and the Railway Men's Club, and many banks and a post office. At the end of the street was the delicatessen. The deli was the place to go to buy rarities like olive oil, thin slabs of real ungrated parmesan cheese and all kinds of weird pink and white marbled sausages. Italians ran it. It's closed down now.

All the banks have been changed into pubs. And where Nelson's Walkaround stores used to be there's an Australian theme pub. Outside many of these places they have bouncers at the door. The bouncers are big men, hard-looking in black overcoats. Their faces are like knives – sharp and threatening.

We're getting tired of walking so much, of being told that the kitchen is closed for the night or being asked how old "the girl" is. We leave Wind Street and try other parts of town. McDonald's is ablaze with lights and we pass it several times, but it won't do. We don't want fast food and fluorescent lights, we want slow darkness and intimacy.

Finally we find a place near the castle. The sign is hand-painted and funky, and the interior looks low budget, but promising. We go in.

The lights are low and every table has a plain white candle on it. The candles all stand in deep stainless steel bowls that look like the kind of dishes which were meant to be dog-food bowls. At the front of the room there's a couple of men setting up a microphone, keyboard and PA. The walls are covered in paintings and posters. Behind the bar there's a big chalkboard listing all the things you can eat. The staff consists of two young men, both tall and thin, clear-skinned and hollow-cheeked. One has a sleek brown ponytail. We gaze hopefully at the chalkboard, but there's something about the place that lets us know we won't get fed. Maybe it's because we can't smell food and there's an unhurried wound-down atmosphere, a sinking into drinking feel.

We ask about meals and they look a little bemused by our request. We've given ourselves away. We're exposed as outsiders. Simon is wearing a suit, a white shirt and tie. I'm semi-dolled up too, in a dress and heels. My daughter looks entirely at home here. She grins enthusiastically. I notice how the young men working here look more inclined to address her than us. As if she is the host, and we are the guests.

I'm tired now. And thirsty. And I'd like a cigarette. I suggest we have a drink and sit down and discuss our plan of action. We sit beneath a big painting of a monkey that is crouching on top of the planet, his tail hanging down, dangling near Australia. He's a wise-looking Chinese monkey. I mean to mention that I was born in the year of the monkey, but someone says something else so I forget. It wasn't important anyway.

My daughter is picking at the candle wax where it's soft and molten near the flame. She's fifteen and grumbles when we won't buy her a beer and so instead she steals most of Simon's lager in frequent greedy sips. He doesn't complain, but I can see a muscle twitch on his jawline, every time he catches her. He's disarmed by the situation, doesn't know how he's supposed to react. And neither do I.

I look at my daughter across the table, she looks beautiful in the soft light. She looks beautiful in any light really, at that age no light needs to be forgiving.

I'm beginning to wonder if this night wasn't a mistake. Whether it wouldn't have been better to stay home. For me to have cooked one of my daughter's favourite meals. To have set the table, and lit candles, and played low slow music, and opened a bottle of red wine. But here we are.

I say that I've never been here before, but always meant to

come. At the front a grey-haired man is testing the mike for sound.

"One, two… one, two," he says in a quiet voice. The room is small and we're so near we can hear him just fine even though the microphone isn't yet working.

There's just two other customers here – a couple who look like they might be students, the girl has dyed red hair and is dressed in a very similar style to my daughter. The boy opens his tobacco tin, rolls cigarettes for himself and her, and they light them, leaning into the candle flame at the same time. It reminds me of the scene in *Lady and the Tramp* when the two dogs are nibbling their way along the same piece of spaghetti.

Another man comes in through the front door. He's carrying a guitar case and greets the other musicians who are still mucking around trying to get amplified.

We learn from a poster that tonight and every Sunday is open mike night. The poster exhorts us to "showcase our talent". I say I could sing "Cry me a River". It's the only song I can do justice to, the only one where I don't forget the words or let my voice go too high and squeaky. My daughter reminds me that she needs guitar lessons and I say yes, yes, we've got to sort that out, as if it was something I keep forgetting to do, but it's not that, it's the money.

We've just about finished our drinks now and we want to stay, but our bellies are empty. We talk about how awful it is that we have to walk out and rob the musicians of three-fifths of their audience. No one has struck a chord yet or sung a note. There's an inch or so of yellow liquid in the bottom of my glass. We decide it's better to go now while the mike is still being troublesome, before the performance has begun. We don't want our leaving to look like distaste, an affront to showcased talent.

It's touch and go. We down our drinks quickly, stand, shrug ourselves into our coats, make for the door.

The man with grey hair makes a joke. He says, well, at least it wasn't my singing that made you go. We apologize, say we'd love to stay, but we've got to eat. Next time then, he says, see you next time.

We shuffle out guiltily, leave him to his almost empty room, his mute microphone.

The night's as black and cold as ever. We walk for a minute then go into the first restaurant we come to.

The food's good there. It's everything it should be. We chat and eat and drink, but there's something missing. We're all feeling it, but none of us mentions what it is.

There's music playing in the background. It's just loud enough for you to know there is music, but it's too soft to be distinct. It's a tape, maybe it's even on a loop. Goes around and around, hour upon hour, like three lost people passing McDonald's for the fourth time. And all I'm thinking about is a lone man standing in front of a microphone. I'm thinking about a room full of empty tables with a single white candle burning on each. I imagine the man standing there and leaning towards the mike, taking a gulp of air. And the air goes down to his lungs, pure and empty, and when it comes back up it's the first note, the first word, of his opening song. And we weren't there to hear it.

Snakeskin Becomes Her

What Jessica wants is to be cured of her incurable sadness. She's walking through town gazing in shop windows and going through rack after rack of clothing, looking for a cure. Maybe she's looking for herself. She picks up a long flowered dress, studies it, then asks herself "Is this me?" She wistfully fingers a pair of pink satin trousers and runs her hand over a tiny mohair sweater that has a little red silk heart sewn over the bosom – "Is this me?"

Maybe sackcloth would be the thing. Or a polyester frock with someone else's sweat stains straining at the armpits and an old wig, stiff and dun coloured. And plastic leather-look shoes and American Tan tights. Maybe that would be a true reflection of who Jessica is.

Tonight she has a date and that's the reason for this flurry of activity. "I have a date," she thinks as she withdraws money from the bank. Money she knows she shouldn't be spending.

"I have a date!" she says aloud in the chemist's as she buys mouthwash and a small bottle of her favourite scent, Poison. When she says this aloud the assistant is supposed to smile, but instead she just stares at Jessica, stony-faced.

Unnerved by this, Jessica goes for a coffee and tries to inspire herself by looking at a fashion magazine. A song is playing on the radio: a hit from a year or so ago. To Jessica it seems to belong to another age, to the time of her youth and innocence. The time before her heart got broken. "Not again," she thinks, frowning at the doe-eyed model's face on the glossy page before her, "*never* again".

She smiles ruefully, adds more sugar to her coffee and turns to the horoscope page. Still humming the song, she drains her cup of its last sweet dregs then wanders out to the next shop. Once there she chooses five dresses, all of them short and clinging, and enters the changing room. She quickly undresses, then tries on the one which is made from a print of silvery snakeskin. She can't decide whether she looks wonderful or absurd in it. She strikes a casual pose, then an artificial, angular one, then she tries to catch a glimpse of her reflection from behind to see if her bottom looks too big. Finally she unzips herself and lets the dress slither like a dead thing to her ankles.

After three hours of shopping Jessica begins to feel panic rise up in her. She should be feeling the beginnings of transformation. She should feel like Cinderella before the ball, but the rats are still rats and the pumpkin remains the same. She would swear that the money in her bag is getting heavier. She's drunk too much coffee and hasn't eaten and her heart is pounding. The day has grown darker and seagulls now reel and scream overhead as they make their way inland dragging a storm in their wake.

The voice inside her, which earlier had been happily pronouncing, "I've got a date! A date!" has subtly attached a question mark to itself. Why is she calling it a date? Why the word that conjures images of neatly combed young men in tweed sports coats who clear their throats awkwardly and loosen their collars in clichéd gestures? It is the language of hot kisses and noses bumping, instead of the one she intends to speak.

She walks on, her knees beginning to feel weak. Sadness is taking hold of her and her last piece of hope is diminishing. She remembers a weather house she had as a child. She thinks about the little figure with the umbrella and its miserable expression as it swung out of one door, while the other figure retreated with her basket of flowers into the shadows.

Then suddenly she is confronted by a familiar face. It is smiling and saying brightly "Jessica! Jessica!"

Jessica, still half submerged in her reverie, makes a weak

attempt at a returning smile.

"How *are* you? Oh it's been ages! How are things?"

The speaker is Vivian, a woman whom Jessica has known vaguely for years. Jessica manages to mutter something in reply about not feeling too good.

"Oh, me too. I've got a dreadful cold." Vivian sneezed then as if to prove it and after wiping her nose continued, "You've just missed Brian. What a pity! He'll be sorry he missed you."

It was strange to hear his name out loud like that, Jessica thought, almost indecent. It was a name she'd only thought about in whispers. She imagines him strolling up the road – maybe even walking right past her and the two of them not noticing each other. She thinks of how he'd have thrown his head back in a delighted laugh if he'd seen her, and of how he would have hugged her close to him, close enough to smell the damp wool and stale tobacco smell of his coat.

She remembers his voice from that morning; the husky half-asleep way he'd said hello when he'd picked up the phone, the sigh of longing in his every word.

Vivian chats away – Jessica has always envied Vivian's ability to make conversation. But Jessica isn't really listening. She is thinking about Brian with his arms around her waist, his lips on hers. She forces herself to listen, to focus and respond. Vivian says "...so Brian threw a surprise party for my thirtieth birthday!"

Jessica laughs and nods politely at this, but inside she thinks, "Thirty!" She can't believe it. But then she's always known that Vivian is older than Brian, and he's twenty five. Jessica herself is a few weeks short of her twentieth birthday. She stares at Vivian's face closely.

Thirty. How can Brian bear it? How can Vivian bear it? No wonder Brian wants to see Jessica tonight. And yet Vivian *is* beautiful. Tall and slender and pale-skinned with something ballerina-like about her face, especially when her dark hair is drawn tightly back as it is now.

Vivian studies Jessica. She doesn't much like her, but

doesn't actually dislike her either. It is generally agreed among their circle of friends that Jessica is a little unhinged. As Vivian watches, she notices how Jessica has a strange nervous tic; a habit of flicking out her tongue and moistening her upper lip. Vivian remembers what Brian had said that morning after he put the phone down. "That was Jessica, she wants to talk to someone. I said I'll go round tonight." Vivian had said sarcastically, "Brian to the rescue, again." He'd got back into bed, put his arms around her and said, "She's just lonely." Vivian had scoffed at this then, but now, noticing the younger woman's unsettling and erratic manner, she thought better of it.

Jessica and Vivian stand and look at one another. Neither of them speaks. Then Vivian gives a friendly sigh and says "Well . . ." and makes to go. Jessica suddenly says, "I was looking for some new clothes. I have to look good – I've got a date!"

"Ah!" says Vivian and she nods knowingly.

Saying it aloud, Jessica finds the phrase is once again imbued with all the triumph and excitement of earlier on. Vivian responds as if to a ten year old. She makes her eyes big and her gestures expansive. "Who's the lucky boy then?"

Jessica doesn't seem to hear this and says instead "Will you come with me – there's this dress I'm not sure about?"

Vivian is flattered to feel that Jessica trusts her. She decides that maybe Brian is right; maybe Jessica just needs a little friendship.

"Okay," she says, "I'd love to. Just lead the way."

As they walk, Vivian tells Jessica about her first date. "I wasn't more than fourteen, but I was dressed up to the nines – a mini skirt, the lot. I had on these hold-up stockings and as soon as I saw him I just ran to him and guess what? The stockings fell down. I didn't even notice! He took one look and said 'Those are funny looking socks'." Jessica doesn't laugh, but merely says "That's not going to happen to me," then gives Vivian an unnerving sidelong look.

They enter the shop which is called What She Wants and

Jessica heads straight for the dress she's tried on earlier. She moves as if hypnotized between the rails of polyester and lycra and Vivian follows, contemplating the ironies of the shop's name and its contents.

Vivian is imagining a sphinx guarding the doorway, stopping all who dare to approach with a "What do you want?" She thinks that if the woman is able to condense all her desires and her needs to a simple request for some cheap slinky garment, then she might gain entry. Vivian can't quite see herself passing such a test, but then she thinks "Who would want to?"

Jessica scoops up the snakeskin dress and disappears behind a curtained-off cubicle. Once inside she quickly undresses; throws her jeans and sweater to the floor with distaste. Then, delicately, with the fingers of a lover, she takes the dress from its hanger and slides the zip down. She steps daintily into the clinging folds, reaches behind and pulls up the zip, which makes a satisfying sound, half hiss, half purr.

Turning her eyes to the mirror, Jessica wonders how she could have been so uncertain about this dress before. She balances on tiptoes and turns sideways, sucking in her tummy, sways her hips seductively and twists her fingers through her hair. Then she leans forward, pressing her chest against the glass, admiring the satisfactory swell of cleavage, and smiles a satyr's smile. Finally, with eyes closed, she kisses a cold, flat, imaginary Brian open-mouthed.

Vivian watches Jessica's feet beneath the curtain, sees the little dancing movements, the pirouettes, imagines the playful vanity.

"Have you got it on yet?"

Vivian's voice seems very near. Jessica opens her eyes and glares at the sound. Childishly she pulls a face and waggles her head, flaps her mouth open and shut in a dumb parody of Vivian.

"Come on. Let's see. Jessica?"

She takes a final look at herself, then draws back the curtain with a flourish. She steps out, twirls and cavorts, "What do you

78

think?"

Vivian smiles her approval.

Jessica sees Vivian reflected just behind her in the big mirror. She's wearing a winter coat and thick tights and big boots, her nose is red at the end and her eyes are pink rimmed and shiny with tears. Jessica imagines Brian having to choose between the two of them. Which will it be? Vivian in her old grannie's coat or Jessica in this beautiful dress and her high strappy sandals?

"So what do you think?"

"It looks really good. I hope he's worth it."

Jessica smiles, lowers her head and as she passes into the changing room whispers, "You should know."

Vivian says brightly "Pardon?" but Jessica has already pulled the curtain across.

"Poor Jessica," thinks Vivian.

"Poor Vivian," thinks Jessica, as she knows how bad a broken heart can feel.

Jessica stands before the mirror again, the long green curtain swaying like a wind-blown forest behind her. She will buy the dress. It was made for her. She moistens her upper lip in that habitual way of hers, flicking her tongue neatly out and back again, then smoothes her hair, narrows her yellow green eyes and smiles.

Settling

In the city you could be free. This is what the man told himself, anyway, as he came down the steps of the bus. He thought that the best way to live life and to cure his problems was to move to another place. He had lived in different parts of his home town, had shared flats in the Uplands, lived in bedsits in Mount Pleasant, had tried lodging with families in Cockett and Killay. He'd then tried out places nearer the sea, in the Mumbles, then wilder places on the north of Gower; the grey marshlands of Penclawdd and Crofty where a man could walk out into the mist and take one last final moonlight swim.

Now he was trying London. He had the address of a friend of a friend who lived in a house in West London. The friend had asked if he could stay there until he got on his feet and they had said fine, so long as he paid something toward the rent and electricity and so on.

No one had given him directions on how to get to the house. Being a friend of a friend, no one really cared if he found the place or not. He would be tolerated rather than welcomed.

Around the corner from Victoria Coach Station he found a café, bought a coffee and sat at a narrow counter against the mirrored back wall. He thought they'd put the mirrors up to make the place seem bigger, but it was disconcerting to find yourself avoiding your own eyes while you ate or drank. He had no problem looking at his own face, but he didn't feel it was the kind of thing he ought to be doing, didn't like the idea of being caught staring at himself. So he fixed his gaze beyond himself at the life going on behind his back at the counter.

After his coffee, he decided to walk for a while, to get acclimatized to London. He was travelling light. He'd pared down his few possessions to almost nothing. He went into a newsagent's and bought an A to Z, but he stuck it in his rucksack and let it stay in there for the time being. He wandered around for a few hours like this. Enjoying the sense of being lost. Of having no past and no clear future. Right now he was just in a narrow slice of time, a bridge between here and there, then and now.

At three he came across a tube station and decided to descend the stairs that led to the ticket office. He spent some time staring at the tube maps and consulting his A to Z, working out his route to the house he'd be staying at. He felt good about the way he hadn't gone running straight there. He'd proved something.

He sat on the tube train ignoring everyone, in the same way that everyone else ignored him. But he glanced up each time the train came to a halt, craned his head to see what station they were at.

A lot of the people on the train were reading things: paperbacks, or the *Evening Standard*, or work papers. He decided he would get something to read next time. It would be part of his reinvention of himself.

He found the house easily, and stood in the porch for a few moments gathering himself for this first meeting before pressing the doorbell. The house was shabby and run down and stood on a busy arterial road. There was a paved drive, and a few dusty-looking shrubs that may have been ornamental at one time, but now they were out of shape and overgrown and invaded with brambles. It was turning dark and looked like rain. He heard the bell ring inside the house. It was a lonely sound.

No one came to the door. He pressed the bell three more times. Then sat down on the doorstep with his elbows resting on his knees and turned up the collar of his jacket. He rolled himself a cigarette and smoked it with bitter pleasure, a wry amusement at this turn of events. Few people passed the house on foot, but there were plenty driving up and down the road, passing before him from left to right, or right to left.

The temperature dropped as the sun went down, and while the porch was sheltered, sitting there on the cold step was causing a chill to creep up on him. He shivered and drew his jacket tighter across his chest. He was young enough though, to still enjoy this. To feel that there was time for a more settled life; one where his ass wouldn't be turning to a numb block of flesh, while his fingers turned blue, while he waited for the arrival of strangers who didn't even know he was coming.

He smoked another cigarette. Checked the time. Stood and pressed a bloodless finger against the doorbell again.

He stared out at the road, noted the disinterested faces of the drivers, saw their mouths move in talk, the fingers drum in tune to unheard music on the steering wheel.

Snow began to fall, at first small meagre flakes, then bigger ones that came with more urgency. He watched it land on the paving slabs just beyond his feet, and saw how after a moment of inert sparkling whiteness, each flake gave up its ghostly presence and melted into nothing but a grey damp patch; a shadow of itself.

The snow wouldn't settle, then.

A man turned into the drive. Walking fast and reaching into his pocket as he neared the door. He didn't see Richard on the porch step until he was a few feet away. Richard stood quickly. Smiled.

The smile was unplanned, but he couldn't help himself. He was grateful to be found at last, to be amongst friends of friends of friends, even if this was in reality a stranger.

He introduced himself, explained the circumstances, mentioned Mike Jones, which was the name of the person on whose hospitality he would be dependent, and the man, shrugging with disinterest, let him into the house. He led him through to a big kitchen at the back. It was not much warmer in here than it had been outside. The man told Richard he could wait in here, pointed out a cupboard that he said belonged to Mike and suggested there might be tea or coffee in there he could use. Then he left him to it, and disappeared to some other part of the house. After a few minutes, music could be faintly heard, drifting down from some warm room, a stranger's small piece of home.

He made himself some coffee, though as there had been none in the cupboard indicated he'd had to take it from someone else's more amply-stocked shelf. What would it matter? It was an accident, he told himself, he was mixed up. It was easily done. Though why he felt the need to lie, even to himself, was inexplicable.

He held the hot mug in both hands, hugged it against his chest as he stood by the window watching the snow fall. The light from the room illuminated the flakes nearest, and they seemed to fall faster that those further way. It was now fully dark out, though it was still early evening. He could just see enough to understand that this room overlooked a back garden. He wondered if it was snowing back in Swansea. It would be as dark. If he was still in Wales right now, he'd be on the bus home from work. He'd be aching from the long day, and aching with discontent. And if it did snow, it wouldn't stick around long. Wouldn't keep the buses from running. Wouldn't stop the world from turning. Not in Swansea, at least.

He heard the front door slam shut and voices; a man's and a woman's, then footsteps on the stairs. He wondered if that might be Mike coming in. Would anyone let him know that he had a visitor waiting for him down in the cold kitchen? A friend of a friend. A friend in need.

The doorbell rang, someone answered it. Laughter echoed through the house, then died away. The door slammed several more times, and while he was certain it was more of the household arriving, he also worried that maybe Mike would come and go again without even knowing he was there.

He felt more distant here in this cold kitchen, than he had on the streets earlier. He felt lost and invisible. More insubstantial than a stranger even; his existence there as temporary as the snow flakes that had failed to settle.

It occurred to him that he could yet undo this process that he'd set in motion. He could put his jacket back on, wash the cup he'd used and put it back where he'd found it. He could lift his rucksack onto his back, go silently though the house, out the front door – closing it quietly behind him – find his way to the tube station again, sit on the train on the other side of the tracks, watch the stations he'd been through once already that day, let their names unfurl for him, one notch more familiar now, but still all a geography of unknowing – Acton Town, Turnham Green, Hammersmith, Gloucester Road, South Kensington. He saw himself almost doing it in reverse, like a videotape rewinding. Himself stepping confidently backwards up the steps of the bus, the door folding shut as he blindly found a seat. The vehicle rolling dangerously into a stream of traffic that was sucked irrevocably back west down the M4 to Wales.

The idea gripped him so strongly that he found himself acting on it; he threw his jacket on, hefted his bag on his shoulder and proceeded to the door. There were lights on in the hall and up the stairs, he passed a downstairs room and could hear a familiar television show theme-song playing. He smelled joss sticks burning somewhere, smoky and over-sweet.

None of it felt like home though.

He opened the front door and would have been gone, but what he saw there held him transfixed.

Snow had continued to fall, and still fell as he watched. It rushed to the earth, an army of fat flakes emboldened by the triumph of their conquest. The world was transformed. Blankets of glistening white lay everywhere and what traffic there was had slowed its pace. He lifted up his head and watched the multitude of flakes fly to him, marvelled at how this swarm of tiny white clouds seemed to emerge endlessly and soundlessly from nothing; poured from the blackness of the night into light, found its place in the bleached world below, and was a single entity once again.

He couldn't remember when he'd last seen snow like this. Had last seen it settle with such sureness. Without so much as a by your leave. As if the world was all for the taking. He wondered how it would look by morning, if it kept falling all night?

After some time he shut the front door and went and waited again in the kitchen. He'd stay. At least until morning.

On the Edge

At first you're not sure if it's easy or difficult – this trick of falling off the edge of the world. Then again you're not even sure how much of an active part you play in it – do you fall or jump? Or even, and this is the hundred-dollar question, do you get pushed?

For me I think it was always waiting to happen. I had too much youthful imagination; spent too much time alone and dreaming. And here's what I dreamed while I played in the sandpit at the bottom of the garden. I would be a lone adventurer like Robinson Crusoe or Gulliver, a lone hero in an alien world struggling to survive against cruel and relentless torments. I would sit for hours, and with a stick for a paddle I would stir at the sand as though it were a shark-filled ocean. I would do it until I got blisters. The pain, it seemed, was an essential part of the game. I had to prepare myself.

Under the August sun, I would paddle my imaginary raft, or stay lashed to the imaginary mast, or hidden in the nettles until my throat was so dry I could barely croak in reply to my mother's lilting call of "Time for tea, darling boy."

So did my childish games usefully prepare me for my fate – as if some part of me knew what misery my future held? Or did these fantasies; my love of pain and introspection, did all that lead me to banish myself most wilfully from the class and comfort of my upbringing?

Cartographers of old used to write at the edges of their charts of the known world, "Beyond this point there be dragons". And dragons there are.

Lily says she has a dragon inside her. She says it is the colour and texture of blood. Sometimes when she talks I can sense the dragon crouched within her belly. But only sometimes. After all, no matter what else I may be, I'm not mad. I know that dragons do not exist. I know that they do not take up residence inside human beings. That they are not made of blood. That whatever it is inside her is not a fire-breathing scaly monster.

Lily fell off the edge of the world when her house burned down with her baby daughter inside it. That's what dragons do, says Lily. Her boyfriend was supposed to baby-sit and Lily had gone out for the evening. She'd wanted a night out, and she felt better than she'd felt for a long time on the bus coming home. Nice feeling, lazy, happy, laughing, singing at the top of her voice with the boys down the back. She got off the bus, went down the street and around the corner to see weird flashing lights. She was so drunk she thought it was a street party with all those people and lights and the glowing house. Then she woke up to the terrible truth. A neighbour in her dressing gown grabbed her arm, pinched her, said to Lily's slippery face, "The babby, where's the babby?" And Lily saw at last the party scene come into focus like changing channels on the TV. The walls of her house a charred black smoking disaster. Someone on a stretcher carried past her. A dead man, but not her boyfriend.

On the lawn, the ruin of her life. The lamp she'd bought last week. A child's red bucket. A kitchen chair lying on its back under a smashed window. Not her chair, though.

No one believed Lily when she said she'd left her boyfriend there to mind the baby. "What boyfriend?" they said and she told them his name was Dave. She didn't know his last name. They were going to get married. She'd known him two weeks.

Lily is a mess of scars. Her left arm carries the brunt of her self-inflicted violence. Lily says she doesn't believe in God. She says her baby's in heaven, but she'll never see her because she's going to hell. Then she says that that's all crap, because the dragon ate God up and she should know because the dragon's inside her.

Then she comes up close and whispers, "Don't tell anyone. I don't want them to cut me open."

Sometimes the dragon idea makes sense. That's usually when I think that she means it as a metaphor, but Lily's not capable of inventing metaphors. Her world is very literal, even if she does view it through a twisting, distorted lens.

I can't imagine Lily ever finding her way back into the world. Can't imagine Lily in a job, or old, or being a parent again. Can't imagine her dead, either. Sometimes though, on a good day, I can imagine all these things for myself. So maybe that's a good sign. The prognosis is healthy. Maybe.

She's given me a photograph of herself to look after. Every so often she asks to see it. "There I am," she says and it's as if she really thinks she is looking at herself in some sealed-off little box, peeping into a safer world where she could dare to smile. "I'm in there, aren't I? And there's the baby. Look."

Lily's skin is white like alabaster. Even when she's dirty, her skin looks pure and pale. When embarrassed she doesn't blush, but grows more ashen as if someone has sprinkled her with talc. I trace my fingers down her throat and over her breasts. Tiny goose-bumped breasts that are scribbled with blue veins like someone's drawn on them in biro.

"Give me a baby," she says sometimes. "I want my baby back." I say, "I can't do that, Lily. Can't get your baby back. Your baby's dead. She's in heaven, Lily."

And Lily says, "Is she?" and hot tears run down her face while I'm kissing her, and I taste salt on the back of my tongue.

Maybe people wouldn't have given Lily such a hard time if her neighbour hadn't gone and got himself killed trying to rescue her. The neighbour was a real local hero type – Territorial Army, lorry driver, four kids and a nice smiling wife who worked in a bakery. He got the baby out first and once he knew she was being seen to, he fought his way into the house again. Maybe he had an idea that this baby was going to be orphaned and would have to grow up deprived of the soft touch, the cushioning love of its mother. He didn't know that the baby was lying on the grass, its little lungs black with smoke, its tiny heart as still and lifeless as a piece of meat on a butcher's block.

In he went through the flames and the thick billowing smoke, with some pathetic damp rag clamped over his mouth and all the time the furious clamour of the fire engine's bell was getting nearer and nearer. But the noise didn't stop him, instead it drove him on, made the moment all the more urgent. And when he came out of the house again it was on a stretcher.

I couldn't be a man like that. I'm a coward, always have been. Though I'm man enough to admit it. One day I'll change. One day I'll have kids and a house and all that.

"Give me a baby," says Lily and I say, "Ssh, ssh," and I cradle her in my arms like she's a child that needs protecting.

"Dave?" she says, "Dave, I want a little baby," and I say, "My name's not Dave. Don't say that, Lily," and she stares at me with this vague puzzled look on her face, as if somehow she doesn't believe me. I get angry then, and I have to tighten my grip around her skinny arms so that I can almost feel the bones and I say, "I'm not Dave, okay? OKAY?" and she says in a whimper that gets on my nerves, "Okay," and I look around the room and wonder what I'm doing there and I want to get out because she's not my responsibility, so why should I have to stay in and mind her?

But sometimes, after I've left her and I go for a walk through town or the park, my reflection catches my eye as it moves past shop windows and still waters. Then I see a creeping, lurking, lying man who looks a lot like Lily's Dave, who looks a lot like me, and I look away quickly, before he can see.

Mistaken Identity

Committee rooms. Committee rooms that are big and blank and impersonal. With tables arranged in a square, circle or rectangle. Chairs with leather seats all placed just so. All facing inwards. All facing each other. Each placed one foot from its neighbour. Twelve inches, very precise.

This is where the world turns. Men and women in suits sit here. They say yes, no, nod sagely. They make amendments, think, talk, jot notes. The walls that surround them are white and bare except for one large portrait which watches them. A man in a suit done in oils. How did he find the time in his busy schedule to pose? Did his wife suggest the green serge suit? Or was it debated on by the committee? And the tie? That's surely the old school tie? Or the Honourable Member's tie? None but the initiated will recognize it. For them it marks him. Points to his importance in the world.

Every time the cleaner comes into this room she bows to the picture. She does this because she can. Because no one is looking. Because no one would care. For her it's become like touching wood to stop bad things from happening. And besides that he looks a bit lonely up there on the wall. His eyes, she thinks, look sad.

The cleaner is eighteen years old and has long blonde pony-tailed hair and a pretty face. She wears jeans, trainers, an old sweater that belonged to her brother and a shapeless overall of baby-blue nylon which she hates. Everyone recognizes the overall. It marks her out. Shows her place, just as the man's suit shows his.

But the cleaner doesn't make the world turn, she just cleans it.

She squirts the world with polish, rubs it with a cloth until it shines. Removes its ashtrays and empty coffee cups, vacuums it, empties its waste paper bins. Places its chairs in their regimented positions, twelve inches between each. One foot. Just so. She doesn't water the plants, that's someone else's job. She doesn't rearrange the tables. Doesn't open or close the blinds. Doesn't touch the picture, except to carefully run the feather duster across the frame. Of the last, she is certain she is doing right, as the supervisor was clear on that point. "Don't polish this," she had said, "and don't scrub it with Vim either." As if. How stupid did the woman think she was?

When the cleaner comes here at night, after all the committee members and the managers and personal assistants and secretaries and word processors and receptionists have gone home, the room is hers. She wheels her trolley up the corridor, unloads the vacuum, the cans of polish, the dusters and the black plastic bags, then carries it all into the committee room and lays it out in readiness. Sometimes the room looks just the same as when she left it the day before. It looks just as if no one had been in there at all. She peeps in the waste-paper bin nearest the door. It's empty. Not even an illicit cigarette end or a suspect tissue. So the room is spotlessly clean. That would please her if she could knock off early, but she can't and so she glances at her watch in order to judge how much time she has to kill.

Instead of vacuuming the floor she runs her eye over it. She finds one tiny fleck of lint, probably from her duster last night, and picks it up between thumb and forefinger and drops it in her rubbish sack. Next she decides to polish the table. This is partly so that the room will smell freshly cleaned, but mostly because she actually enjoys doing this. Sometimes, when she is in a particularly indignant mood, she sprays words in large letters across the table. Words like WANKERS or ARSEHOLE. Today she's in a gentler frame of mind so she sprays a large heart and inside it writes "Olivia loves..." She hesitates then – who does she love? – and settles for a question mark.

Olivia. What a name to be stuck with. She blames Olivia de Havilland for this indignity. Olivia de Havilland, Gone with the Bloody Wind and her mother's over-romantic imagination. She gets the duster and draws it over her words in large sweeps, turns her love into a beautiful shine. A shine that will reflect the faces of the committee members. A shine which will mirror their eloquent frowns, their expensive shirts. Their ties will make a river of colour with their stripes of blue and emerald and scarlet and gold. As if they'll notice. But it passes the time. Offers a little variation, a stand against the tedium.

Olivia does corridor Q which consists of one committee room, five offices, two public toilets, male and female, and two private washrooms, also male and female. She does the corridor itself which is the most boring part, being straight and long. The equivalent, she thinks, of motorways for long distance lorry drivers. This work takes three hours out of her life each evening, from Monday to Friday. On Saturday she works in the market, selling bread, a job she's had since she was fifteen. On Friday and Saturday nights she works in the Quayside Nitespot as a barmaid. Olivia's friend Sue works in the casino and says she'll try to get Olivia work there. The pay's not much better but the tips are good. "Oh," says Sue, "the tips. You wouldn't believe it." Olivia does believe it, but all she can do is wait and hope.

Olivia's been cleaning corridor Q since she started this job back in June. It's now the beginning of December and she no longer wonders what the rest of the building is like. She no longer yearns to see corridors A to P – leave alone clean them. All she wants to do now is get a better job and fall in love.

More than any other, the big committee room with its floor-to-ceiling windows and its starkness makes her aware of the changes in the weather and the seasons. In June she watched the sun sink while she cleaned the room and went home in the last of its light. Now it's dark when she arrives and the windows, with only blackness behind them, have become enormous mirrors. Out there, beyond the brightly-lit room, another room hovers like a twin world. The cleaner can see herself, a little figure in a blue overall. A nobody. It reminds her of that poem about nobody which the teacher had read aloud at school. It had been the first time she'd been touched by words in the alien language of poetry. She remembered how she'd felt a sweet lilt of recognition in the pit of her stomach, and breathed an involuntary sigh, and then Dai Thomas had said, in his belligerent, full-of-it way, "Yeah, but she's not nobody, is she, Miss? She wouldn't be in the book if she was no one." The teacher – one of those new young hopeful ones – had just wilted into silence, while Ed Thomas had given the class an evil leer and rocked his chair back, his arms resolutely folded, proud to be an angry zero who could see through all the lies.

This December the weather is mild, but in the office, black heat blasts from the radiators regardless. Olivia's feeling uncomfortably hot. She hasn't been sitting still, coolly talking, calmly shuffling paper, she's been pushing around an industrial-size vacuum. She's been rubbing and lifting and shifting and lugging and scrubbing, and she's hot.

The overall is sticky so she unzips it and takes off her jumper. She takes off her shoes and socks, hopping about to keep her balance. She was going to keep the overall on over her T-shirt, but that's even more uncomfortable. The clammy nylon sticks to the skin of her arms and neck, so she throws the hated garment through the door where it lands near her trolley. Now that she's just in her jeans and T-shirt she feels much better. Not only cooler but also much more herself.

She checks her watch. There's still time to kill. She goes to the corner of the room and stands, back erect, head and arms held high as if she were about to dive into a pool. She's aware of the carpet hot and bristling under her feet. Of her breathing and her stillness. Then she throws the top part of her body down and forward. Her hands reach the floor and her legs arc upward and for a moment she hovers there like an acrobatic toy. Then she flips down into a crab, but she can't quite lift herself into the standing position again, so she collapses instead. Next she throws herself into four perfect cartwheels, one after another, which bring her to within inches of the window.

Momentarily dizzy, Olivia faces her reflection, remembers that this glass is not a mirror, but a window, imagines reports of gymnastic goings on. Imagines the supervisor's sarcasm, her own humiliation. She frowns, then cups her hands around her eyes and presses her brow on the cold glass and stares out. The town is spelled out in a constellation of street lights. Over the far hills, patterns of yellow dots traverse the night. Nearby four towers of bright light illuminate the football ground and closer still, across the car park and the dual carriageway, the prison offers its broken rectangles of half-light to the stars, to her eyes.

Unlike the little terraced houses with their downstairs glow and flicker of blue TV, and unlike the flats with their patterns of occupation and emptiness, the prison has only two states. There, all the cell lights are uniformly either off or on, regardless of the occupants' needs or desires. Olivia stares at the curtainless windows and wonders who lives beyond them, what men they imprison. She doesn't imagine rapists or murderers. She knows that they are there, but thinks instead about the beaten men, the half-innocent, the young, gone-wrong, never-given-a-chance men. Men like her brother Jake. But Jake is in Strangeways in Manchester. If he was here she'd be able to visit him. She'd be able, maybe, to wave to him.

She counts the windows. There are ten across by five down. Fifty windows. Fifty souls. Fifty narrow beds. She imagines a man like Jake. He's probably in there for drugs, like Jake. Probably only sold stuff to his friends. Then found he suddenly had a lot of friends, like Jake. Then no friends, also like Jake. She'd been to see him once since he'd been inside. The journey took four and a half hours and someone on the train, an insipid woman in a pink shell suit with three screaming children, had sat with her and attempted a conversation. "Visiting friends?" she'd asked. Olivia had just said "No" and turned away.

Olivia looks away from the main block of old grey stone to the newer red brick extension and counts the windows again. Eight across and only three down. And then she sees him.

He's standing on the second floor at the third window from the left. His arms are outstretched, holding the bars at shoulder level. She can't see his face, the light behind him makes him a silhouette. But she can read his sadness in that pose. He's a crucifixion of misery. He doesn't move.

Does he see her?

Tentatively, she raises one arm and makes a slow arc at the night.

And slowly, like a strange mirror which responds only after a mis-timed delay, like a star whose light reaches earth long after its last flicker has died and given way to endless night, the figure raises its arm in an echoing arc.

In the prison, the guard, who has been standing by the window in the staff room yawns and, as is his habit, fingers the heavy metallic bulk of the keys that hang from his belt. He smiles as he thinks of the girl in the office block opposite.

The night hangs between them, a curtain of blackness. Far away and long ago, unnoticed by either of them, a nameless star gives its last violent pulse of light, shrinks down to the volume of zero and becomes a black hole that swallows everything within its pull.

The Game

In the gallery two men were standing side by side. For a long time they stood in silence, each with hands clasped loosely behind their backs. Each with the weight of their body on their left leg while the right was flexed. Although from different generations the face each wore was the mirror of the other. They could have been brothers, but they were actually father and son.

The picture that held their gaze was a large work of the seventeenth century. Its subject was a game of cards and showed three players around a table engrossed in their sport. By standing in front of it, the father and son seemed to close the circle of figures. The son's red waistcoat matched the scarlet of the central woman's hat while his father's suede jacket echoed the tawny hue of her dress.

The father leaned closer, eager to break the silence. "So, what do you think?"

"I'm not sure really. What do you think I should think?"

"I don't want to put any ideas into your head about this. I just want your first impression. Tell me what you see."

"Well, that's easy. The painting."

The son spoke in a tone of frustration. He hated games. He knew there was something his father wanted him to see and was torn between stubborn refusal to obey the abstruse demand and fascination with the mystery his father seemed to be offering him.

"Look, this isn't a trick. There isn't a right or a wrong answer. Just look at the painting and tell me the first thing that comes into your head."

As he studied the painting the young man thought back to a time when they had stood like this in front of another painting, Holbein's "The Ambassadors". As a child of ten he had stared glassy eyed at the two men with their props of oriental carpet and curious instruments, and had dismissed it as just another dull old painting in a wilderness of dull old paintings which he had been forced to endure in an eternity of museums and galleries. Then his father had pointed out the strange diagonal shape that crossed the picture.

"It's a skull. Do you see it?"

They'd bought a postcard of the work and his father showed him how you had to hold it in a horizontal position close to your eye to see the skull. He could still remember the delight he'd felt with that discovery. It opened up another world for him. After that he'd looked for other secrets, other hidden things. He searched for faces and figures and words and other signs in every painting he saw. Studying in minute detail the smudge of a cloud, the fold of a gown. Then as he learned more, he became fascinated with the difference between this artist's cloud and another's. Was the gleam in that jewel achieved with an impasto or scumbling? Did this picture belong more truly to the Expressionist movement or the Fauve? His knowledge had overtaken his father's in leaps and bounds. For a time their joint trips to the galleries became a battleground in an intellectual power struggle between them. Or rather, it seemed that way to the son, who felt a need to shake off the role of awe-filled pupil. He felt the picture they now stood before was yet another skirmish in their war of knowledge.

"Why don't you just tell me what it is about this that you find so remarkable?"

The father noted with some pain the harsh impatience growing in his son's voice.

"Alright, it's this. I know I don't have the benefit of your education. I'm no expert, but there's something about this painting that seems out of place."

The son had felt that too, but was determined not to be the

first to express it. He nodded his agreement.

"Take the background for example, it seems too black, too harsh. There's no attempt to give it depth, to imply, however loosely, that there is anything beyond the figures. It makes them look like cardboard cutouts!"

"Perhaps that was the intention of the artist. Perhaps he wanted to show them as shallow, as time wasters?"

"Alright then, what about the figure of the young man on the left?"

"What about him?"

"Well good God. Can't you see it? He doesn't even look like he belongs in the painting."

"That's true to some extent. But there could be any number of reasons for that."

The father shook his head and folded his arms.

"For example, the figure may have been finished by an assistant."

"Well, the assistant must have been untrained or drunk or both! I would have expected even an assistant to follow the style of the whole work. Can't you see how out of place he is with his swarthy skin and gaunt bone structure, compared to the other moon faced players?"

"But he's there isn't he? Or are you suggesting that he got bored with being a bit player in a marriage-à-la-Hogarth and strolled down here for a change of scene?"

Further down the room a guided party approached noisily. The father gestured towards them. "Looks like we've got company."

Their shared distaste for the drone of the guide's practised speech and the empty nods and perfunctory laughter of the group gave them an excuse to escape. They left for coffee. That night the son had a strange dream. It was something to do with his father and a fly. It flashed through his mind when he awoke, but the dream seemed only to exist on the edge of his mind. He was puzzled and tried hard to remember what exactly it had been about. But it had fled, leaving only a dim shadow. He hated losing dreams like that; forgetting them except for a confused flavour. It was like smelling something familiar that couldn't be placed. That was the trouble with foreign travel and unfamiliar beds, dreams always came on curious wings.

Over breakfast they made plans for the day and came to an unspoken agreement that some time apart might be a relief to each of them. The son decided on a lazy day of pavement cafes, whilst the father set out to stroll around the left bank book-shops, leafing through erudite and dusty volumes.

The streets of the city were hot; the air heavy with the enclosed traffic fumes that dried the throat and made the head throb. The son went in pursuit of the narrowest streets: private, down at heel places empty of tourists. He stopped here and there, drinking a coffee or a Pernod, sometimes reading his book but mostly just watching the people go by.

By late afternoon, feeling empty bellied and light headed he came across a tree-lined square whose cool greenness seduced him to rest. Settling himself beneath the spreading branches of a cedar tree, he closed his eyes. He slept fitfully, the fire of a midday hangover burning his senses, the incessant buzz of a fly entering his dreams.

When he awoke he felt a sickness rise in him and tasted vomit at the back of his throat. His head swam and he blinked. He struggled to pick out his surroundings from the greying twilight of the trees around him. Gradually he came to his senses and stretched, yawning, then checked his watch. He was late for supper and back at the hotel his father would be waiting, angry and impatient and worst of all, hurt.

He arrived in the dining room out of breath, yet not quite as late as he thought he'd be. There was no sign of his father, so he stood catching his breath, considering the choice between a quick shower or a much needed hair of the dog before dinner. He chose the dog and was making his way towards the bar when he bumped into his father, who looked him carefully up and down and frowned.

"You're not going to the bar are you?"

"Well, you weren't in the dining room, so…"

"You look like you've had enough."

"It's the heat."

"Just the heat?"

"Well, no, maybe I did get a bit carried away."

"Hungry?"

The son smiled and shrugged, a child again; glad of the adult who reminds you to eat. He began to turn towards the dining room but his father caught his arm.

"I rather fancy a change."

They left the hotel and crossed the street. A breeze chased papers and leaves around their feet and the moon began to show itself, paper thin against the blue black sky and gathering clouds. They chose a cheap restaurant, gaudy with chequered tablecloths and discoloured reproductions of Degas' ballet dancers.

When they were settled and had ordered their meal, the father produced a small paper bag from his pocket and set it artfully on the table between them.

"For you."

The son hesitated, his father had never been one to give endless presents for no good reason. He looked at him quizzically.

"What's in it?"

"Why don't you open it and see?"

He peeled back the sellotape which was sealing the bag and feeling embarrassed at this public gesture of affection, he reached inside and pulled out a book. On its cover was a reproduction of the painting they had seen in the gallery. The son leafed through it enthusiastically, taking brief glances at every page or so to give himself the flavour of it.

"You like it?"

"Yes, of course I like it."

He held his book fondly, running his hand over the pearly surface of its cover.

"It's beautiful."

"I'm glad you like it. He's quite a remarkable painter, isn't he?"

The waitress approached with steaming bowls of soup and the son hurriedly replaced the book in its bag. They ate with a hunger and a happiness that brought a soothing silence between them. Afterwards they drank and talked of the past, each bringing to the other a store of memories that had been forgotten. They laughed at stupid things as lovers do.

That night the father and son drunkenly hugged each other on the landing outside their rooms. The father retired with an Alka Seltzer, the son with his new book.

The room was swimming as the young man closed the door. He put the book on his pillow and, staggering a little, undressed himself before falling heavily on the bed. Propped on one elbow he opened the book and stared at the image of a blind beggar, whose mouth was open in a grimace of singing whilst his hands clawed a musical instrument. The painting drifted in and out of focus and his eyelids were weighted by the dim light and silence of the room. He fell asleep with the book on his pillow while its substance became his dreams.

He was a child in the dream. An angry tired child who must stand still. His father shouted orders at him. "Don't move boy, you'll ruin it. That's it. Now turn your head a little more to the left. Stay like that."

His limbs ached and trembled and he was fearful of his father who towered over him like a god in a long red robe. He began to cry. "Father, I can't. I'm tired. I can't do it."

His body shuddered and his father raged. Then he fell as in a faint, but the fall was endless, his body seemed caught in limbo between his upright pose and the timber floor at his feet. It was then that he knew he was dreaming and he struggled with the weight that seemed to be pressing down on him. He resurfaced from sleep, drenched in sweat and shivering.

He said nothing of the nightmare the next day. He was

afraid the sub-conscious betrayal would shatter the happy peace between them. They walked by the banks of the river, enjoying its slow progress as it cut through the heart of the city. Both felt fragile and abashed by the previous night's indulgences; they spoke in formal tones like vague acquaintances. The son carried within him a small but nagging resentment for his father's cruelty in the dream.

They visited a cathedral and stopped to purchase and light candles, though neither was a believer. Each was enraptured by the pagan ceremony of the act and by the incandescence of the massed flames which flickered with the bright fires of others' faith. The son sat staring for a long time at them, considering their yellow glow and trying to dispel the cramped tightness he felt inside.

He was remembering more of the dream. There had been a candle and he had been forced to cup his hands around it until his fingers were nearly burnt. His father was a painter and he had to pose for him dressed as the child Christ or as an angel or whatever. He realised that in the dream he seemed to have adopted the poses from the paintings in the book, while his father had become the creator of the paintings and his own dreamchild's agony.

He felt a flood of bitterness towards his father and looked up to see him standing some way off, gazing at a stained glass window which depicted the pieta. His stomach knotted and adrenaline soared through his veins; he stood and began making his way towards his father. The cathedral lurched around him like a great ship.

"Are you alright? You look terrible." His father's hand was resting lightly on his shoulder. "Come on, let's get a breath of fresh air."

The son watched him uncomprehending for a second. He saw a fly alight on his father's temple and a hand brush it away. They walked together into a heat which waited like a wall beyond the great wooden doors. The young man was sick. Violently and suddenly it gushed from his mouth, red with yesterday's wine. Splashes of it landed on his trousers. People passing craned their heads to watch the torrent whilst screwing up their faces in disgust.

The pair returned to the hotel, where the son took a shower and brushed his teeth, swallowing minty globules of toothpaste to dispel the bad taste in his mouth. His bed had been made up with fresh sheets and he lay down and enjoyed their crisp coolness before sinking into a deep and purifying sleep.

He awoke refreshed, his mind was unclouded and he felt as sharp as a well-honed knife. He called room service and ordered cheese, bread and coffee. He studied his face in the mirror, sweeping his hair back and turning sideways in order to catch sight of his profile. No one could doubt that he was his father's son. He wondered where his father was, but decided against seeking him out; instead he decided to enjoy the solitude of his room. From down below he could hear the steady and monotonous hum of traffic, while outside his window, pigeons scraped along the roof tiles and gulls screamed and swooped. He looked at the sky, the sun was still shining but the clouds were the deep blue grey that warned of an approaching storm. He settled at the table with the book and broke off a hunk of bread, then went from page to page, sometimes stopping and going back to look at a previous painting in the light of one he had just seen. He puzzled over it; it wasn't just that one of the man's paintings was strange. His entire lifetime's work was unfathomable. Some of it was masterly; superb and otherworldly, like nothing he had seen before, yet other images seemed like the work of some ham-fisted amateur. They were crude and out of proportion and lacking in any sense of beauty or reason.

He finished his coffee, then slowly flicked through the pages to the reproduction of the blind beggar. He propped it up against the wall and rocked back in his chair, gnawing on his bread. There was an overall impression of stone in its colouring, broken only by the scarlet slash of a feather cap lying at the man's feet. He leaned closer, wiping the grease from his hands on his trousers. Something caught his eye, a blue-black speck on the hurdy gurdy the man was playing. He peered closer. It was a fly. He smiled. It seemed to him like an insect caught in the amber of time. Like an Egyptian cat or a cave painting of a buffalo. It brought the ordinariness of the past to him. The fly made the painting perfect, it spoke of transience and humanity.

He remembered how earlier that day in the cathedral a fly had alighted on his father's forehead. How a hand had brushed it away. How up until that moment he had felt an irresistible urge to punch his father. How the hand that gently brushed the fly away had been his own.

The Diving Girls

Me and Annie. Annie and me, always together, always friends since back before even memory kicked in.

We're stepsisters, though we hate that name because of the Cinderella connection, where there's nothing but ugliness and cruelty and that's not how it is with us. We don't share blood, but there's something else we share and that's the sea. So we call ourselves water sisters.

Our town is a small one that nestles on the edge of the Cambrian coast and wherever you go there you're never more than ten minutes away from the sea, and that suits us well.

In the summer we get up with the sun. We put our swimsuits on first and then clothes, any old clothes on top. We don't care how we look, we throw on old jeans, tracksuit bottoms, raggedy Indian skirts with elasticised waists, then flip-flops or trainers and any old top. Then we get our towels, big bright beach ones, or when all these are wet, smaller pale pink ones from the pale pink bathroom. We each lay a towel on our beds and on top we place our goggles, suntan lotion, pants and bras. There is something sad about the last two items, because those signal the end of our pleasure, the return to the elements of air and earth, when we'd really rather stay in the water.

So we roll these up with a kind of mock formal gloom, then we fly out of the house and walk towards the sea front. When we catch sight of the sea, our pace quickens and often we run the last hundred yards until we come to the promenade and the steep steps down to the pebbly beach. We shed our clothes carelessly, kick off our shoes and throw our towels down. We hobble bare foot as fast as we can over the pebbles and to the sea.

Even on the coldest days we think that the best way into the water is the instant plunge and then the thrashing gasping race to the pier and back.

Me and Annie. Annie and me, not related by blood, but by salt water; just like mermaids.

She is fifteen and I am sixteen. Her mother, a divorcee married my father, a widower when she was five and I was six. Our first meeting had been, aptly enough, on those endless sands at Rhossili. Her mother and my father were perfectly suited to one another as they were both earth-bound creatures who sat on the sands fully clothed. They would remove their shoes, though and come down to the water's edge while we joyously splashed and capered.

Today is overcast and not as warm as a day in June should be, and so we're the only swimmers on this stretch of beach. We've swum to the pier and back and now the cold water feels almost warm against our skin, and so without saying a word we know it's time that we swim further up to the wooden jetty. We clamber onto the platform and from there take it in turns to dive from the high timbers that support it.

I watch Annie dive. She is magnificent, a shiny flying fish, a sea nymph.

Then Annie watches me. I take my time, imagining how I look, my body straight and sleek, a muscular extension of the wooden post. I adjust my goggles, then lift my arms so that it seems as if the tips of my fingers are the tallest things around. The top of the post is barely big enough for me to put my feet side by side and yet at that moment it feels like the most solid place in all the world. I lift my body up even further, my feet arching with raised heels so that I am on tiptoe, then I flex my knees and finally throw myself into the dive. I enter the water like an arrow and cut through it, continuing down until it's time to arc my body upward toward the light again. At the surface I tread water a safe distance away from the post. Annie is already up there, smiling and shimmering, waiting for me, waiting for the perfect moment, and then she too dives again and disappears beneath the waves with barely a splash.

This is happiness. It is joy and purity and innocence. It is easy. It is Annie and me. Me and Annie breathless and dangerously jelly legged when we eventually wade out of the water with the morning gone and the sun beginning to break through the clouds. When we've got our breath back we begin to struggle out of our wet costumes. It is no easier; despite all the practice we've had, the towel still occasionally slips and our swimsuits seemed stubbornly glued to our damp skin.

Our only consolation at this point is the thought of the hot lunch that will be ready for us as soon as we get home. Annie retrieves her watch from her shoe and I notice that she sways giddily for a moment as she looks at it.

"Whoa," she says, "head rush." Then, "We're late. It's half past one!"

Without another word we begin to run up the pebbles towards the promenade.

It doesn't feel that late. Three hours is usually enough to make us tired and hungry and drive us back home, but somehow time has tricked us, or seems to have.

"Mum'll kill us," she shouts and I notice that she isn't wearing her shoes but carrying them. She breaks into a giggle and I laugh too and speed up, because with my shoes on I know I can lick her. I'm just a few yards from the steps when I hear a scream. It's so sudden and so raucous a noise that at first I think it's a joke, but then I hear my name being called and there is a wail of pain in the word. It is an indignant, plaintive noise.

I stop and turn and at first I don't see her because I'm looking for a standing figure, one that asserts itself against the blank canvas of the sea and sky. But then she cries out again.

"Ow!" she cries, "oh, ow!" and I see her lying sprawled on the pebbles and first I laugh because she looks so funny lying there, but then I see that her face is drained of colour. Her hand flutters up in a helpless wave. The hand is daubed with something red and gleaming. I run to her, my feet slipping and twisting on the pebbles so much that I almost fall too. I reach her and kneel next to her. She is writhing about in pain and there is blood everywhere. So much blood that I can smell it and taste it. It's sickening and I feel my stomach lurching. Both of her legs and feet are smeared with crimson and there is a dark scarlet pool blossoming on her pale blue skirt.

There is so much blood that I cannot tell where it is coming from.

"What have you done?" I ask, feeling panic rise in me. "Where does it hurt?"

Annie is speechless with pain. She struggles to sit up, then puts her bloodied hand to her face, increasing the horror of how she looks as she is smearing the stuff around her mouth, over her cheeks and chin.

"Don't!" I say and just as I say it she vomits violently. Most of it spills on the pebbles, but it is also in her hair and down one side of her T-shirt.

I feel so helpless. It seems all I have to save her is words. Silly words and stupid questions, and a foolish and misplaced loyalty that renders me reluctant to leave her side. There are other people on the beach but they're out of earshot. There are people milling about on the promenade, but they are as distant and unreachable as the figures in a Lowry painting.

Finally between low moans, Annie finds words and arranges them into a need, a solution.

"Mum," she says. "I want Mum."

I don't hesitate for long. I stand up and look at her. I seem to tower over her. I am all strength and speed and health, while she is broken, an old toy washed up on the shore, a bundle of red rags with arms and legs and head just loosely attached.

"I'll get Mum," I say and I take off running. I climb the steps three at a time and race along the promenade dodging tourists and day-trippers, weaving through their incautious dallying at speed. I run past the shops and cafes, past a policeman strolling pleasantly and dutifully up the main road. I pass some girls from my school. They flash into my consciousness like a snapshot. I see that they are sneering, laughing at me, but nothing matters now except for Annie.

Me and Annie. Annie and me. I'm racing down Great Dark-gate Street with her blood on my hands. With her life in my hands.

I reach our house and tear through the door screaming "Mum, Mum!"

Everything is so normal here. There is the inviting smell of onions frying and the radio is playing and a housefly is worrying the window, flaying at it then buzzing off angrily to complain to the ceiling, the light bulb. Mum isn't there. I call her name and run to the bottom of the stairs and call again.

All the time I imagine Annie dying. Annie slipping away, her blood pouring over the pebbles to be washed away at high tide. And Annie herself being carried off by the hungry waves, pulled down by the undertow, back to her element to swim forever.

I go back to the kitchen and skim my eyes over the room looking for clues as to where our mother is. There are onions and sausages over a low flame on the stove. From the radio a woman's voice sings an aria, it's something like Madame Butterfly. I look at the old school clock on the wall, it reads ten to twelve and that confuses me. It's as if I've entered a dream or woken from one and now truth and reality seem to hinge on the accuracy of this clock. If this is the correct time then what happened on the beach hasn't happened yet. If it hasn't happened, then I can stop it from happening. But then why am I here? Why am I alone? And where is Annie? Where is Mum?

It occurs to me that perhaps none of this is quite what it seems. Or that I am not quite what I seem. Maybe it was me who died and this is what it feels like. It feels like real life but you keep running and searching. You sense there's been a tragedy and you want to solve it, but everything is misjudged and misunderstood. I stare at the clock and nothing makes sense and the fly is having the same problem with the windowpane, no one can tell him why he can't just fly through it.

Mum comes into the kitchen then, through the back door; she's singing along with Madame Butterfly with a plastic laundry basket propped on one hip.

"Just in time," she says when she notices me.

I do not know what to say. There's a moment that slips by while I gulp air and the fly buzzes about, a black angry flying demon.

Mum is still humming the aria, but she's more restrained now that there's someone listening. She puts the laundry basket down, then jiggles the frying pan.

"Where's Annie?" she says, and I hear such confidence that all is well in the world in her voice, such innocence.

No words will come, so instead I slowly lift my palms to show her the blood, to display the stigmata that unbalance the world.

She understands at once.

"Where is Annie? What's happened? Where's my baby?"

I suddenly feel like a bit player in this drama. As if now I have delivered my message I can retreat backstage and watch the rest of the show with detachment. Maybe this is because I have passed the script into the safer surer hands of an adult. Or perhaps it's because she called Annie "her baby" and I've recognised a deeper truth about us. Seen at last that I never was, never could be "her baby".

She seems so angry with me. She is shaking my shoulders and asking me over and over where Annie is, what has happened.

Me and Annie. Annie and me, we are no longer one and the same. We are not equal. I am whole and she is broken and this is her mother, not mine.

My eyes slide back to the old school clock, its round stripped-pine casing and cold enamel face. I am in shock, I suppose and that makes me say the wrong thing at the wrong time.

"Is that clock right?" I ask.

I look at her face, expecting her to answer, expecting her to understand the significance of the question, but she only shakes me again and says, "Pull yourself together!" and delivers a hard stinging slap to my left cheek. This does the job and I manage at last to blurt out the information she needs and she goes to the phone and rings the emergency service and then my father.

We drive to the beach and by the time we've followed the twists and turns of the one way system it takes longer than if we'd walked. There's an ambulance parked near the steps and two men in uniforms are carrying a stretcher towards the vehicle. They carry it solemnly. It reminds me of the way a coffin is carried during a funeral and because of that I think that she's dead. My Annie dead and because of me, the ugly spiteful stepsister.

But she isn't dead, just sleeping. Or not sleeping, but unconscious.

Mum goes with her in the ambulance and I have to lead a policeman down to the beach and show him where it happened. It's easy enough to find the place, though the blood is not so red now, it's turning to rust like something that should never have been immersed in water.

The explanation for her injury is there too, shards of broken glass and the heel of a bottle with jagged edges like the teeth of some monstrous predatory animal. There is blood on this and a sliver of flesh that is already turning yellow.

The policeman picks it up gingerly and sucks air over his teeth. "Nasty," he says. "Your friend was unlucky."

I want to tell him that she is not a mere friend, but a sister, yet suddenly that does not seem true and so I am silent.

Me and Annie. Annie and me, by late August we're swimming again. On land she still has a limp; her body has acquired an ungainly sideways lollop. It is not that pronounced, but what is noticeable is that she's lost her grace, her poise. In the sea though, she is still magnificent.

Under water I swim towards her and she smiles at me bravely, offering me consolation and sympathy for all I have lost. For all she has gained.

The Blackberry Season

It's said that no blackberries should be picked after the eleventh of October because that's the day the devil tried to get into heaven. Old Gabriel was waiting at the gates and he wasn't a man to be easily fooled. He threw that old devil out. The devil went falling through the sky; down, down, he went through the stratosphere and ionosphere, past snail clouds and cirrus clouds until, thump, he landed in a thorny blackberry bush. The devil got so angry he spat and spat and didn't stop spitting until the whole bush was covered with foamy phlegm. The berries turned mouldy and bitter, and ever since that time, each year on that day, they do the same.

So when Linda said that I ought to make some friendly gesture to Catherine to show that there were no hard feelings, I decided that a home-baked pie might be just the thing. Blackberries, of course; it was the season. To make it extra special I decided to pick the fruit at night; midnight on the eleventh.

I crept into the garden with my torch and my colander and prayed that no one would see me. The night was cold. A familiar crisp, frosty smell met me and brought back memories of bonfires and fireworks. It was the smoky scent of October and November and December; those magic months of strange ritual. There was a night for witches and a night for burning effigies. There were days of angels and mistletoe and pine trees and a night of Auld Lang Syne. Now, in the garden, I would make my own bitter-sweet ritual as I picked the shining clusters of fruit.

The moon was full and silvery and I found the berries easily in its light. The colander was soon full and I laughed a little at myself as I carried it back through the nettles and brambles without a single sting or scratch. I had no belief in my sorcery, the whole business merely amused me. It was a happy revenge. I could have cooked her an apple pie and spat in it myself but the devil's spit was better. Besides, to spit in it myself was too low, too dirty, and too much what she'd expect of me. This would be enough, this friendly gift baked with loving care. I thought about our meeting, how she'd hug me and say, "Oh Susan, dear Susan, I'm so sorry things had to happen the way they did!" and all the time she'd be gloating inside like a cat that's killed a great, fat rat. She was the queen of control, she switched smiles and tears on and off like an actress in a long-running show, her eyes glistened and her teeth flashed in a smile, but the feelings had long ago been forgotten. She was a surgeon with emotions as finely honed as a scalpel and like a surgeon she knew just which one to choose at the appropriate moment. So, from caring concern she'd move to nostalgia, "It's so sad, it was so good at the beginning. We were all so...." then her lip would begin to tremble and she'd try very hard to smile. At this point of course I should also be on the brink of tears and I should hug her fluttering, sparrow shoulders and weep like a baby, but I won't. Instead I shall just say that it's all in the past now and what the hell, with other such platitudes. Then, I would give her the pie.

The house was dark and silent when I entered, the hall lights had been switched off and everybody, I supposed, must be in bed. It was warm in the kitchen as I'd turned the oven on in preparation for my night's baking. I put on a tape of Wagner's "The Ring" for a bit of company, then rinsed the fruit under the tap and thought some more about Catherine. I remembered how nice I thought she was when we were first introduced: I turned to find a small, blonde woman, beaming at me, her hand outstretched toward me. We shook hands.

"I've heard so much about you. You must be very proud of the work you've done for the gallery," she gushed. "Jenny tells me it was you who arranged the 'Man-made Images' exhibition. I thought that was marvellous, so pertinent to current feminist discourse and art theory."

I smiled; I just liked the pictures. I also liked flattery.

I turned off the tap and found myself grinning at the blackberries. Remembering that I had no reason to smile, I felt the old anger rise up like indigestible dough swelling inside the walls of my chest; choking me. I sifted the flour into the bowl and added a pinch of salt. I crossed the kitchen, opened the fridge and stared in, wondering what Catherine had been doing these last few years and what it was I needed in the fridge.

No doubt she'd been steadily climbing her ladder of success, leaving lesser mortals by the wayside. She was what you might call an exceptional woman, a high achiever.

Margarine. I drifted back to my bowl and dropped a cold chunk of it into the flour; clouds drifted up, dusting my sleeves with their ghostly particles. Catherine's parents had encouraged her, nurturing each interest or small talent as it showed itself. There had been piano lessons and day trips to the Tate and National Gallery. Many a happy hour had been spent with Daddy in the Science Museum and many a happy week in Greece and France and once, the USA. She had ballet lessons for the grace and discipline it would bestow on her in later life. And her very own pony so that she could learn to conquer and control.

I rubbed the fat into the flour and the salt into my wounds. I wished her ladder hadn't crossed my path. Did she mistake me for a snake, I wondered? A slippery snake that might drag her back to square one?

How did it happen? How did I fall from grace and glory? Was I a cat who thought she could not only look at kings and queens, but live among them?

My anger grew as I mixed water into the mixture, stirring it and moulding it.

The child in me was wailing, "It isn't fair!" and I kneaded the pastry and pounded it like dough. Having ruined it, I sighed, dropped it in the bin and began again. It must be the best for

Catherine, only the very best would do.

At first we'd had very little contact. Put simply, she dealt in words and I in pictures. It wasn't that I couldn't deal with words, it was more that in my view each painting or photograph existed in its own right without the need for the props of words. Perhaps I relied too heavily on intuition, yet more often than not it paid off.

My intuition let me down as far as Catherine was concerned: I'd trusted her completely. I'd told her things about myself that I could barely tell to my best friend. She was like that; she had this power, she could draw out even the darkest secrets. And yet all the time she withheld her own truths.

One evening I was working late, hanging the pictures for an exhibition that was due to open the following afternoon. I had propped each painting against the wall and I was sitting in the middle of the room considering how well the arrangement worked. Catherine came in quietly, smiling and nodding approval as she looked around.

"You must be tired."

I shook my head, "Not really."

"It looks wonderful. You do have an eye for this, I'm sure I couldn't do it."

"It's the paintings that are wonderful. It doesn't take much skill to hang them."

"Are you planning on staying much longer? I really fancy a drink and I'm almost done in the office."

We went to a pub near the tube station and found a table away from the darts players and the jukebox, and we chatted about the gallery. Then, somehow, I found myself telling her all these very private and difficult things about my life. She made a big deal of everything. Telling me what a hard time I'd had of it and what a strong woman I must be. I told her about my mother dying and how my father drank, and about the evil step-mum.

I was careful this time with the pastry. I got sick of Wagner and put on some Johnny Cash instead. The songs he sang were so mournful they always had the effect of making me feel quite happy.

I sprinkled flour on the formica surface of the table and began to roll out the mixture. There is something very satisfying, creative even, about rolling out pastry; taking a mis-shapen lump and turning it into something flat and thin and delicate.

I wondered what kind of cook Catherine was. I knew she gave smart dinner parties, but that didn't mean she was a good cook. I suddenly realised that I was still looking for something I could outdo her at.

Pathetic.

I greased the dish and draped a limp sheet of pastry over the bottom. I spooned the fruit in and sprinkled it with sugar, then peered closely at the berries. Something seemed to move. I poked around but could distinguish no wriggling maggoty thing hiding there. What did it matter anyway? I suddenly felt ashamed of myself. What did I think I was doing? She was still making a fool of me. Still making me prove to the world what a rotten crawling parasite I was.

I picked up one of the blackberries and brushed away the sugar. I could see nothing wrong with it. I popped it in my mouth, almost fearing its poison, my poison. It was a little overripe – its taste was blandly innocent. I ate another. This time it was not ripe enough and was hard and sharp. I ate another and another and another, until they were all gone. I thought about going into the garden to fetch some more, but I couldn't be bothered. In the cupboard I found a tin of cherry pie filling that I'd been saving for a rainy day, and I opened it. It was thick and gelatinous and over-sweet, and dropped from the spoon in great cloying globules. I covered it quickly with the rest of the pastry and popped it in the oven.

I thought about how it had all started. How we'd had those chats in the pub and more often. She was so interested in what I had to say and so keen to know. "She took photographs? I thought she was just a model, a beautiful hanger on!"

So I'd tell her all I knew.

I gave her a potted history of women artists of the world in twenty easy lessons. I lent her my favourite books and told her which exhibitions were worth seeing. I thought I was her teacher. Then, one day at a meeting, I'd been talking about a show we'd been hoping to put on later that year when she interrupted me.

"Excuse me. I'm sorry, but did you just say that Tina Modatti was the lover of Alfred Stieglitz? Don't you mean Edward Weston?" Everyone turned to look at her. She was smiling benignly. I stood silently wondering how she could know more than me. She continued, "Or perhaps you were referring to Georgia O'Keeffe, who was the lover of Stieglitz?" By then I had lost my thread entirely and couldn't remember who I was talking about or why. "Or Dorothy Norman, also a lover of Stieglitz?" She paused, then added in a throwaway, sardonic tone, "Quite a guy, old Stieglitz." A ripple of laughter went round the room, I blushed and stuttered and tried to continue the talk, but the momentum was gone. Jenny, bless her heart, suggested we all have coffee. I never did finish that talk and the idea was forgotten.

The smell of baking filled the kitchen as I cleared away the bowls and wooden spoons and weighing scales. It was getting late and I began to feel tiredness washing over me in great waves. I heard the front door slam and loud voices in the hall. I felt caught in the act, guilty of what, I did not know.

When I next saw Catherine she said nothing about the incident at the meeting. Instead she asked me if there were any good books on a photographer she'd just heard of called Diane Arbus. I said no. Why should I feed her information if all she was going to do was use it against me? At home I had three excellent books on Arbus, and a quantity of magazine and journal articles, and home, I decided, was just where they were going to stay.

Paul and Richard came into the kitchen to make coffee, they were swaying about and laughing.

"What's that lovely smell, Susan?"

"Ooo, smells great, Susan. Give us a bit."

"No, it's for a friend."

"Oh, we're not your friends then, eh?"

"You're drunk," I said, taking it out of the oven, all golden and steaming.

"And you're a great cook."

Flattery always gets me. The pie was delicious.

Hatred can burn inside you. It can stick to the roof of your mouth like hot jam. It will hurt for days. Best thing to do is spit it out as fast as you can.

I felt a bit mean about the Arbus books. After all I had made the mistake about Tina Modatti's lover. Catherine had been right to correct me. I started to think I should say something like, "Who were you asking about yesterday? Did you say Abbott or Arbus?" Then she would repeat her question and I could offer her the books and salve my conscience.

I realised that Jenny was right – the past was the past. What happened couldn't be changed or rewritten. Poison pies and devil spit and spitefulness didn't help me then, but brought about my downfall; maybe it would do the same now.

If only I hadn't lied about the books. I just couldn't believe it when I heard about the new exhibition and who was going to organise it.

"Susan. Guess what?"

Jenny had come rushing into the gallery, nearly falling over herself in her excitement.

"What?"

"You know the New York Museum that put on the 'Two Centuries Two Hundred Women' show?"

"Yes."

"They're lending us the Arbus collection."

"What!"

"It's brilliant, isn't it? Catherine got it. I can't believe it. It'll be one of the best things we've ever done!"

"Arbus?"

"Yes, Arbus. You know. Oh no, Catherine said you'd never heard of her. Well, she's really important. I'm surprised you've never heard of her. Anyway must run, I've got to tell the others."

She turned to leave. I wanted to say that I did know. That I knew everything there was to know. That I'd loved that woman's work for ages. But no words came.

"Oh, by the way, you don't have to worry about all the background stuff and research. Catherine knows it all, so she'll be curating. See you."

I went to bed with a plan to cancel the meeting with Catherine. I decided it would hurt too much to see her, to hear all the wonderful things she'd been doing, to smile and smile and swallow my pride and anger.

What I dreamed that night I do not know, but I woke feeling happy with the world and cleansed of the past. I would meet Catherine and I'd smile real smiles. She couldn't hurt me anymore. I was sure of that.

I decided that my friendly gesture would be to buy her lunch. That would be enough; an unplanned, uncalculated offer of friendship.

We met at a wine bar of her choice. I sat at a table near the back and after ordering a glass of the house wine I settled down with a book. She was late as usual, but after twenty minutes I glanced up to see her moving briskly towards me, smiling and nearly sweeping everything from each table that she passed.

"You look wonderful."

She bent and put her cheek next to mine and kissed the air at my ear. Then she sat down and waved an arm at the waiter who was suddenly and miraculously moved to an attentiveness he had not previously possessed. While he fetched the champagne which she insisted she was going to treat us to, she rummaged through her bag and produced a large gift-wrapped package. The bow wafted elegantly as she passed the be-ribboned box over the table to me.

"Oh Susan, I hope you don't mind, I just had to get you a little gift. For old times. I want you to know how much I think of you. You're very special, you know?"

I took the parcel from her, too shocked to protest. Too

embarrassed by the unequal exchange to even thank her. Irony and contradiction danced in my wine-fuddled head.

"Well; open it," she urged, "only be careful."

She watched me intently as I untied the satin bow and peeled back the expensive paper to reveal a box.

"Oops. Keep it upright!"

The thing inside the box felt heavy and cold. I struggled to open it. Catherine watched over me like a beneficent mother hen. She clucked as I struggled to free my gift, and cooed when it was finally released.

I placed it on the table before me. It was a beautiful, and clearly expensive, glass dessert dish, and inside it was an artful swirl of pale lilac and syrupy purple.

"It's a creme anglais with a blackberry and Kirsch coulis," she said sweetly. "I made it myself. I even picked the berries... specially... just for you."

Siriol, She-Devil of Naked Madness

My name is Siriol. I am old now, but when I was young they used to call me the She-Devil of Naked Madness, and mad I was too, but never entirely naked. In those days such things were not permitted. I've come to understand that things are different now and that my act, which was then considered outrageous, would now be thought tame. This saddens me somewhat, as I, through my life's calling, was ostracized. Decent people would have nothing to do with me, though enough of them came to see me in all my glory. Indeed they loved me, but only as long as the rope which bounded the ring separated us. If I ever should, in the course of a bout, break that boundary, flying through the air, broken and bejewelled to fall amongst the sawdust at their feet, they would cheer and bundle me back under the ropes and onto the four cornered dias that was my rightful place. It was the same with my everyday encounters with them, except for the absence of cheers to herald my removal and their shunning of me. Instead it was letters to the council, minor complaints about noise and strange comings and goings and despite my innocence in most matters of immorality, they would win and I would find myself homeless and friendless once more.

Of course, looking back I can see that I was foolish to think that I could have had a normal life; living in a normal home, beside such normal families. In those days when I walked down the street even the trees would twitch and draw themselves back in disdain, sensing my disguise, seeing through my ordinary clothes which wrapped themselves too thinly around my beautiful body; all muscle and power and woman flesh.

Even as a small child, I knew I had a calling. I remember one day standing in the kitchen – I couldn't have been more than five – my mother was standing at the sink shelling peas or some such other womanly task, and I was chatting away as all children do, excited with myself, feeling assured and secure and loved. I told my mother that my mind was made up – I knew what I was going to be when I grew up. "What's that, darling?" she said, full of both love and distraction as only mothers can be. I put my little hands on my hips and stood just so, my dainty feet in their pretty red sandals thrown apart, my head held high.

"I'm going to be a lady wrestler!" I said.

She, at this, stopped what she was doing and turned to look at me, her hands held limp over the edge of the sink, a pod half empty of peas cupped loosely in her palm. Her mouth fell open, then she laughed with delicious surprise at her youngest offspring's pronouncement. I tried out a frown, "I am you know!" and she shook her head and went back to the peas.

That memory has stayed with me all down the years. It was a revelation I suppose. My first act of defiance, and yet one which could not have been undone or thought through and therefore halted. Before I spoke those words I was innocent of their effect, ignorant of any stigma attached to such a declaration. Only speaking the words into the hot air near the oven, whilst my mother stood silhouetted against the steamed up windows, light streaming around her, could tell me of their power and change me forever.

I liked to think of myself as a kind of priest or nun of the burlesque – if you'll forgive the analogy – I too had a calling, and while that calling did not demand I shun the ordinary side of life, that world shunned me. And of course, like nuns and priests I wasn't entirely alone in my calling, there were thousands like me: vaudeville players and trapeze artists and showman boxers and freaks and vagabonds and clowns and strippers and wrestlers. Of course we were all very rarely in the same place at the same time – well imagine what a sight that would have been – by the nature of our work we tended towards the nomadic. Like wandering Jews searching for the chosen land yet all the time trapped in Babylon. There was no changing any of us; we were what we were, like it or not.

Take a character like my old friend Loelia for example; she was in her day the world's most tattooed lady. Now you might say that's a very strange thing for a young lady to do. You'll feel perhaps, that the getting of tattoos is not quite on a par with a lady being unfortunate enough to grow a beard. That this was not the same as being a freak of nature – people would say she chose her path, made her indelible bed and must therefore lie on it. But my feeling was that she was born with those tattoos. Oh they weren't on the surface of course, that would be ridiculous, but I think that in some way they were always there beneath the skin, etched like fate in the plan of her life's course. She had the desire, you see. The vision of what she could be. I've heard men talk of sculptors who, when they begin with a big old lump of marble or what have you, they see beneath the mis-shapen stone a beautiful woman, a cherub, an angel's wing and all they have to do is chip away the excess and there they have it – the thing is released. So it was, I believe, with Loelia.

It was Loelia who first met the artist. He had a way with him that you couldn't resist, such a strange little man and yet so blessed with intuition. Well, that's artists for you I suppose.

Anyway, our Loelia met up with him mud larking about at the Isle of Dogs. Not very auspicious circumstances, I'll admit, but they were both there searching for treasures. She was hankering after some ancient coins – a bit of exotica to jangle about her person and maybe flog down the Old Kent Road if things ever got tight. He was shoaling up a booty of old driftwood and other useless curios.

Now as Loelia had been born and raised to mud larking, so

much so, you might even say she'd been born with a clay pipe clamped between her infant gums, she eyed this new face with suspicion. He meanwhile, eyed her with curiosity and she said, more than a little longing. But then Loelia was always reading deep desire in the eyes of men, even if they were blind, so her word can't be taken with certainty. Anyway, there she was, barefoot by the Thames, dress tucked into her drawers, her arms caked in mud wielding a shovel, bucket and deep frown, when up he walks bold as brass and says "Madam, if you'll forgive the intrusion, I couldn't help but notice your tattoos and quite frankly, I'd very much like to paint you."

"Oh, saucy!" she replied, thinking no doubt that this was a new come-on line.

To cut a long story short, after some negotiations she agrees and off she goes to get herself immortalized or, as she put it "demoralized" – which, of course, would be quite a different kettle of kippers. The next thing you know, she's brought this chap around to my lodgings and he's eyeing me up and down like I'm a prize sow and saying he'd be ever so grateful if I'd be so kind as to sit for him and so on. Now despite my experience in some matters – such as how to deal with the spivs and pimps and fraudsters of the world – I was still quite naïve and no-one had had the good sense to warn me about artists or tell me how they should be dealt with.

Anyway, as I said, he did have a way about him. He wasn't all airs and graces as you might have thought, but very down to earth and funny. So there we were, me and Loelia and this little artist chap, having a drop of the strong stuff from the chipped tea cups my charming landlady had grudgingly supplied, when he jumps up and says "Elvis Presley!"

Loelia and I watched as he leaned over the bed to reach my framed and signed photograph of Elvis. He read the inscription out loud, "'To Siriol, with love, your friend Elvis Aaron Presley.' You met him then?" he said, and I could tell by the way he said it that he must have been a big fan of Elvis, which I must say endeared him to me greatly.

I went and stood by the bed and gently took the photo.

"Oh yes," I said, "I met him. In Germany it was. A town called Freiburg, if I remember rightly. He was Private 53310761 and I was the assistant of a magician called Wild Wolfgang – the lady-wrestling business suffering an unexplained slump at that time. Three times a day I got sawn in half – it didn't half give me backache, I can tell you. Anyway, after the show one day, there was tremendous excitement backstage and eventually I caught on that this was due to the presence of some chap by the name of Elvis. I'd never heard of him, so when he's brought up to me and presented as if he's some sort of royalty, I said, 'Well, mister I don't know who you are, but if you're here to fight some war, I'll wish you luck but don't expect no sailor's farewell or other nonsense, because despite the circumstances of my career my mother raised me to be a proper lady.'

"Well, he laughed and called me ma'am and then of course, it was explained to me that Mr. Presley was himself in show business and had always hankered after meeting a lady who was brave enough to be sawn in half."

Of course, that broke the ice straight away and before you could say 'Blue Hawaii' we'd got 'Hound Dog' on the gramophone and were having a knees up and laughing until we were fit to burst. After a bit we were all sitting around and Loelia was giving the artist a geographical itinerary of her various tattoos – what they meant and who did them – when he suddenly turns to me and says "You haven't told us about your tattoos, Siriol." I told him that was because I didn't have any, so he asks me then, what would I have if I did have one. I had to think long and hard on that one as it wasn't anything I'd ever considered.

Loelia started suggesting various things she thought might appeal to me – sailors and hearts and roses and the like, but I just shushed her, I was trying to think of something unique and special to me. Funny thing was, my mind had gone completely blank. Put on the spot like that, as it often happens, the more you try to think the worse it gets. The only thing that did occur to me was a nice rasher of bacon, but of course I was probably just a little peckish after all the jitterbugging and sherry, and who'd want to spend eternity with a rasher of bacon stamped on their rump I want to know?

The artist was watching me all this time and I didn't half feel daft. Why didn't I just say a mermaid or a cupid and have done with it – it was only a bit of fun after all. Then Loelia excused herself, saying she was just off to powder her nose and no sooner was she out of the door than he leans towards me, real cozy like, and says quietly – or if you will "sotto voce", "You and I should form a pact. We could be like blood brother and sister."

I moved along a bit, making sure I put a good yard of candlewick bed cover between us and slapped his knee and told him I didn't know what he could be thinking of.

"No," he said, "It's nothing like that. It's just that I thought it was something we could both do – get a tattoo – that is. The same tattoo."

I looked him in the eye and tipsy as I was, I could see that this was something terribly important to him, so I asked what he had in mind. Just at that point who should come barging back in but Loelia screeching something about me getting "Cut here" and a dotted line tattooed around my waist. As if I would! Then she has a good old laugh about how Wolfgang would look when he saw it, and leant back in her chair, shut her eyes, opened her mouth and snored like a fog horn in a pea souper.

We both sat and looked at her slumped in the chair for some minutes. It was what you might call a pregnant silence and then he said, obviously sobering up a bit, "Well, maybe it's a foolish idea." By then, of course, I'd not only come round to the idea, but felt a little disappointed that he'd had a change of heart, so I said, "Oh come on, you haven't told me what you thought we could do."

"It's a homage," he said, "a sort of vow of devotion."

Now over the years I'd tended to grow rather slack in my

devotion; prayers and church-going hadn't seemed the thing to do in my profession, but having been raised by nuns to be a good Catholic girl I was hankering after something sacrificial and symbolic. Looking for something of the hereafter to jolly me along.

"But, what?" I found myself saying, "What are we going to get?" I was so excited by now, that I hadn't even noticed how I'd slipped from the world of "what if" to the far more definite "lets-do-it-now, I'll-just-get-my-coat".

"Come here," he said patting the three feet of pink candlewick between us, "I'll whisper it."

I shuffled closer, so that we were sitting cheek to cheek as they say, and he cupped his hands to make a tunnel between my ear and his mouth and whispered the magical word.

The word sent a shiver through me, running like a cold hand down my back.

Loelia awoke suddenly, said "Venus de flaming milo!" smiled to herself, then went back to sleep. What she was dreaming of I don't know, but you can be sure she was overdoing it even in sleep!

He and I grinned sheepishly at each other, then nodded and silently shook hands. The next thing I knew, we were blinking in the sunshine of a Tulse Hill afternoon and marching side by side and arm in arm towards a tattoo studio I remembered visiting with a nautical friend.

By now, it was getting towards three thirty and the pavements were full of tired-looking mothers tagging their children home from school. We half sang, half hummed Heartbreak Hotel as we weaved our way along. I felt almost as though I was in love, but that wasn't the case and never was. We took a right off the main road, went down Brixton Water Lane, passed the school at Effra Parade and took a left into Railton Road and then we got lost.

We'd stopped singing and I was beginning to get a headache. He kept tugging at the collar of his sweater and occasionally he pulled a paisley bandanna from his trouser pocket and mopped his brow. My hand was getting sweaty, tucked under his arm and the wool of his sleeve was scratching at my knuckles. I pulled my hand free and stopped walking.

"I'm sure it was here."

"Well, it's not is it?" There was irritation in his voice and he was red-faced and frowning.

"Well, there's no need to be like that," I said, my voice growing louder with each word. "It was your stupid idea anyway."

"It wasn't a stupid idea," he insisted, looking at me as if it was the first time he'd really seen me.

People were staring at us, craning their heads towards us as they passed.

I took a deep breath, "Look it was here a few years ago, it must have closed down or moved somewhere else."

He looked at his watch and said, "It was a stupid idea wasn't it?" He looked so sad and so old suddenly. The colour had drained from his face and his skin seemed as molten and fragile as candle wax. Beneath his beard and moustache I noticed how small and pink his mouth was; like a child's. He said it was getting late, he'd have to go home, he had work to do. I said, "What about the painting? Do you still want to do the painting?"

In reply, he murmured something I couldn't catch. I took it to be no. He said then that he'd go and catch a bus, and asked if I'd find my own way home. I nodded. We parted without another word. Before I took the turning back to Railton Road, I paused and watched him walk away; he didn't look the same, the spring had gone from his step. He was like a small old drunken sailor with loneliness in every bone.

As I watched I knew I'd lost something and yet at the same time I knew it was not the man, but a part of myself which was lost; that bit of me he had wanted to paint. I suppose he'd seen some quality in Loelia and I which we couldn't recognize in ourselves. Then I saw his hand reach into his pocket and the bandanna flashed briefly and brightly through the air like a firework. He turned the corner and was gone.

Many years after that, when I was past my prime and the days of the high life were over, I would often spend my days in the art galleries, libraries and museums of London. It was an escape from the boredom of home and the demands of the electric meter which like a baby chick had an ever-open mouth. In the winter especially, when my poor old bones ached from the war wounds of my wrestling days, I would be up at dawn and out with my thermos flask and sandwiches for a day of warmth and culture. One particularly bitter day when there was snow on the ground and still more snow, hanging heavy in the sky and blanketing the senses with its unrelenting cold, I took refuge in an unfamiliar gallery on Cork Street. I was adept by then, at passing for an eccentric aristocrat, but still I was careful not to sit too long or show too much disinterest in the art. I did my crab-like walk of reverence, eyes to the walls and the paintings there hung, all the time soaking up the minutes of heat. Sometimes, despite the seeming absorption of my vision, my eyes would be blinkered by my thoughts; the swarming days of yesteryear, the faces of the long dead and my lost self. This day, my major sensation was the biting cold of my feet and my need to resist the temptation to stamp them to get the circulation going again, when before me like a ghost swam the face and form of Loelia. She had one bright blue eye, while the other was a smudge, half erased. Over her body were glued, as though in a child's scrap book, words and faces. Above her head was painted the legend "Loelia: World's most Tattooed Lady" whilst below her stockinged thighs it read "Entry" and beside that there was a pointing hand. So this was it. This was Loelia demoralized, as she put it, at last.

I remembered again, that day in Tulse Hill, the bandanna pulled from his pocket, bright as a magician's bunch of paper flowers, and felt that dreadful loss more sharply than ever before. I kissed my fingers and blew the touch of my lips to Loelia's, and shuffled on past fairies and women in bouffant hairdos wearing black brassieres and scenes from *Alice in Wonderland* and my feet grew warmer and set my mind free from their physicality. And then I met myself. A shock. A chunky round-faced girl, half naked in a bikini and sailor's cap. I was blonde and bejewelled and like Loelia, had one sad eye, perfectly painted whilst its partner was a blur. Above my head there was my name. My legend. My tag. My label.

I felt giddy, drunk even, though it had been years since I'd touched a drop. He *had* painted me, then. In all those long looks he'd been fixing me, taking in my shape and details, remembering the particulars of colour and costume, setting me in the amber of his eye.

Everything was there; the glass ruby in my belly button, the star of rhinestones between my breasts, my bright red calf-length wrestling boots. But there was something else too. Something extra, an embellishment. There on my left thigh, his torso disappearing under my bikini bottom, was the unmistakable lower half, hips a-quivering, of Elvis Presley, king of rock and roll. I opened my winter coat and fingered my skirt, gently lifting it until I could see my leg and for one instant, through my tights I caught a glimpse of tattooed feet and tattooed jeans, the knees bent in a frozen gesture of dance. I felt set free. The promise was fulfilled.

Over the Rainbow

It's a late afternoon one Saturday in July and I'm sitting on the bus with my boyfriend Simon. We're going up and up these improbable Welsh hills on which a council estate has been flung, endless, concrete-coloured and inhospitable, when Axe gets on the bus at Nimbus Parade. All the streets are named after meteorological phenomena, like Sunshine Street and Lightning Close. Which is in keeping with the ancient road that links them all, Rainbow Hill.

Axe recognizes Simon, and sways and smirks his way up to the back where we're sitting. Behind him there's a girl I've seen around the town a lot. Her hair is orange. Not ginger, but the bright artificial shades of a cheap plastic toy or a traffic cone. There's no colour in her face except for two grey smudges under her eyes and a light sprinkling of reddish sores around her mouth and over her forehead.

I've seen her before on better days, so I know she's pretty. Today, however, something has gone slack; her eyes are dead and the lids are droopy and puffed. She's wearing a long satin skirt that at some time must have been a delicate shade of baby pink, and through it you can see that she's wearing black knickers. Her arms are bare and white except for a tattooed pattern of black geometric shapes that encircles her wrist.

They sit down heavily next to us on the long bench. I can see the driver turning around to check them out before he drives off. I know that as he looks at me and Simon, and Axe and the girl, he sees one and the same thing. We are now a foursome of dangerous misfortune.

Axe leans across me to talk confidentially to Simon. He smells strongly of beer and cigarettes, with an unmistakable undertone of vomit and bad breath and stale sweat. He's hissing loudly, "Got any gear? Got any stash?" and Simon is shaking his head "no" and smiling to show we're friendly.

Axe got his name from an incident when he was fourteen. He took an axe to school and planted it straight in the headmaster's desk with a single blow – whack! Maybe he'd be inside for murder now, if it hadn't been for the fact that he'd embedded it so deep, he couldn't get it out again.

Axe ignored our negative response and went on to the next part of his proposal.

"Listen. We got no cash, yeah, but we got some stuff, you know. We can trade, yeah?"

The girl meanwhile had been sitting trance-like, staring straight ahead. He nudged her, "Mags. Oi. Show them the stuff we got." Without looking at him, and as if her eyes were fixed by some beatific vision that hung in the air somewhere between herself and the driver's compartment, she passed him a large velvet shoulder bag.

Simon was still trying to say he wasn't interested, and a woman from the seat in front of us, after a few furious glances over her shoulder went and sat further down the bus. Axe noticed none of this, but rummaged around in the bag and then produced some cassettes still sealed in their plastic shrink wrap. These he dropped into my lap, before grinning and breathing straight into my face.

"Check out them sounds, girl. 'S good stuff. 'S good music for loving and chillin', yeah?" Then he began a laugh, which quickly turned into the sort of cough that seemed to shower spit and phlegm everywhere. A woman with a toddler got up from two seats away and went to the front of the bus, despite the fact there were no empty seats down there. She stood, holding the child and glaring back at us all with unadulterated hatred in her eyes.

"There's over a hundred quid's worth there, man."

I looked at the cassettes in my lap. They were the bargain sort that'd cost around two pounds each in a newsagents. I could see a Hank Williams, a Brenda Lee, a male voice choir and a Sixties compilation.

I imagined Axe and Maggie dancing in some empty and derelict room, his thin body, shivering and grubby, moving twitchily to the music, while she hung onto him and stared at nothing, and in the background male tenors and baritones swooped and soared, singing "Bread of Heaven".

Seeing that we weren't impressed with his music selection, Axe thrust his arm elbow deep into the bag again, this time pulling out some bars of mangled-looking chocolate, a pack of half-frozen chicken pieces and some ugly little figurines of wizards and dragons and castles each set around a chunk of crystal. He selected a couple of the gothic monstrosities and passed them to Simon, then sat back and popped a cigarette between his lips, lit it and mumbled, "Take your time, yeah?"

Simon smirked at me and shrugged his shoulders, holding a figure in each hand.

The smell of cigarette smoke didn't take too long to waft up to the driver. Suddenly, halfway between stops and precipitated only by the shrill hiss of the air brakes, the bus came to a standstill. The driver got out from behind the wheel and I noticed for the first time how extremely tall and well-built he was; he probably supplemented his bus driver's wage with work as a bouncer. He rolled his sleeves back to reveal forearms which reminded me of Popeye's.

"Oi," he said, jutting his chin in our direction before lifting his thumb and gesturing towards the exit.

Everyone turned to look at us. Small children pointed and people muttered to each other. I started to stand up, but Simon caught my arm and pulled me down. Axe, meanwhile, sprawled back more comfortably in his seat, his legs stretching almost three rows down the middle aisle, and blew smoke rings in the air.

The driver stared at him. You could see in the man's eyes

that he was imagining all kinds of horrible tortures for Axe: thumbscrews and electric shocks to his genitals, or maybe just tying him to the rear of the bus and dragging him through the streets until he was half dead.

Axe was staring back. I tasted something metallic in my mouth and was suddenly aware of my heart beating heavily in my chest. The driver took a few steps up the aisle, then stopped and addressed the passengers, giving the moment a pantomime quality. He explained that "this had to be done" and that "the journey would be completed shortly" and finally, ominously, he warned people to "keep the kiddies clear".

Simon had pressed his back against the window and I found I'd pressed myself hard against him, leaving a gap of a foot or so between Axe and me. I felt unreasonably angry with Simon for not letting me take the seat by the window. Axe was still sprawled in the middle seat enjoying his cigarette, his mouth clamped over it in a leer.

No one made a sound apart from a gleeful thirteen-year-old who was shoving handfuls of crisps into his mouth and watching the scene with abandon. It seemed that at any minute the driver might rush at Axe, and I found myself anticipating the thrashing of bodies and the dull crack of fist against bone.

Before any of that could happen there was a voice; soft and sweet and as breathy as Marilyn Monroe's.

"S'cuse me, s'cuse me." The voice was Maggie's. She stood and I watched as she daintily lifted her long skirt to thigh length and stepped neatly over Axe, then picked up the velvet bag and put it over her shoulder. Next she scooped up the cassettes from the seat where I'd off-loaded them and leaning over, plucked the two figurines from Simon's outstretched hands, and dropped all this into the bag. Finally, she lifted Axe's hand and pulled him like a large sleepy child behind her down the bus.

"S'cuse me, sorry, s'cuse me...." She squeezed past the driver with Axe in her wake. They climbed off the bus and every head craned around to watch their progress. The crisp-eating kid shouted "Bleeding junkies! Why don't you go and O.D!" and the driver tutted and shared a few words about "scum like that" with some women at the front.

Maggie and Axe passed by our window. Neither of them looked at us. In the sunshine they looked even paler and sicklier than before. Maggie, I suddenly noticed, was barefoot and seemed to glide over the pavement as if it were wet sand. They were still holding hands and except for each other, seemed entirely alone and alien in the universe in which they walked. The bus started up and they disappeared over a scrub verge heading in the opposite direction from their house.

I turned away from the window and looked at the place where they'd been sitting minutes before. On the floor where Maggie's feet had been, placed side by side as if some invisible woman wore them, was a pair of red leather dance shoes. The sort with a button fastening and a sturdy heel.

I leaned across and picked them up – they seemed brand new. The size, 38, had been stamped on the inside, and was still clearly visible. I was a size 38. I slipped off my sandals and put on the red shoes. Then I lifted each leg a little so that I could see the effect. I liked the way they made my legs look, the calves curved and plump like a dancer's and the skin of my foot, pale and fragile, disappearing under the red leather. I tapped out a light two-step of my own invention on the floor of the bus. Simon was deep in thought and noticed none of this, his gaze fixed instead on the passing streets and far-off hills.

I put my sandals in the place where Maggie's shoes had been. This act seemed to have a particular significance, as if one pair of shoes must be substituted for another.

We reached our stop, which was right at the end of Rainbow Hill: the place where the sprawl of the council estate ended and the country began. As we walked to our house, I looked down at the bright flashes of red that carried me forward, and I found myself smiling like a little girl. These shoes, I guessed, would take me to places that poor lost Maggie could only ever dream of. Maggie was a sleeper who'd never wake and her dreams would always be barefoot. For myself, I knew where I was going.